7-26-07

You hold in your hands the realization of a dream.

Enjoy

Love,
Alexis Rhae

THIEF OF THE GALLOWS

Alexis Rhae

Bloomington, IN  Milton Keynes, UK

AuthorHouse™
1663 Liberty Drive, Suite 200
Bloomington, IN 47403
www.authorhouse.com
Phone: 1-800-839-8640

AuthorHouse™ *UK Ltd.*
500 Avebury Boulevard
Central Milton Keynes, MK9 2BE
www.authorhouse.co.uk
Phone: 08001974150

© 2007 Alexis Rhae. All rights reserved.

No part of this book may be reproduced, stored in a retrieval system, or transmitted by any means without the written permission of the author.

First published by AuthorHouse 3/6/2007

ISBN: 978-1-4259-8941-5 (sc)

Library of Congress Control Number: 2006911306

Printed in the United States of America
Bloomington, Indiana

This book is printed on acid-free paper.

Prologue

LANCASHIRE, ENGLAND

The boy sat on the dusty ground with his back to the brick wall below the window. The wall made him feel stiff and uncomfortable, but then so did everything else about the place. He hated that house, with its white washed walls and sweeping grounds. It belonged to his uncle, his pompous, overbearing uncle, whom he had only met once before in all his twelve years. That` meeting had been the day of his birth. He poked at the ground lazily with a stick as he listened to the voices floating out of the window above him.

"I simply can *not* have him here!"

"But what shall we *do* with him, m'lord?"

"Send him to an orphanage. He's only a gutter whelp like his mother; no one will miss him."

The boy tensed with anger at this remark. *Hold back,* he told himself, *I'll be gone on the morrow.* Over the past few days, the days since his mother's death, the boy had made a plan. He had lived all his life on what little scraps of food his mother could provide, spent nights sleeping in cold ditches. But no longer. He was going to run away and create a new life for himself from the ashes of the old. He was determined to pull himself from the depths of the vile, loathsome gutter.

The majestic grandfather clock in the hall struck one in the morning as the boy crept to the kitchen. Clothed in rags with a haversack slung over his shoulder he prepared to embark on the great journey of his life. He began to fill the sack with various items. A knife, bread, salted pork, and an apple all went into the sack. These were followed by some squares of cloth, a needle, and thread for patching his rags. After some fishing about in the pantry, a small flask of wine was thrust in as well.

As he was packing these meager supplies, the boy wondered what he would do when these ran out. He had no skills for any trade, he wouldn't find work easily. The boy tried to remember what his own father had done for a living. Actually, he could hardly remember his father at all, as the man always seemed to be away on business. But they had been well off, he and his mother. Somehow his father had just never been there. Then, without warning, there was no more money. He and his mother were forced to sell their home.

He began to realize that he was going to need money to get started. His uncle had a lot of money, but to ask would be to admit that he was running. His uncle would refuse anyway. *Besides, stealing isn't really stealing if it's for the sake of necessity…is it?*

He stole into his uncle's dressing chamber. Uncle Marcus had left his silken purse on the dresser. Carefully, the boy lifted out and counted each glittering coin. The sum was ten gold sovereigns. His hands were shaking as he wrapped half of the coins in a handkerchief. He tried to make himself believe it was because he had never touched gold before.

The boy stepped out of the room and shut the door silently behind him. He peeked down the hall and saw the door leading to the room that had once been his mother's. He shivered involuntarily, but could not stop his feet from drawing him toward it.

He opened the door and felt the rush of stale air against his face. It was as if the room itself had died along with its former inhabitant. He stepped forward slowly and ran his hand along the bedside table. Unexpectedly, his hand contacted with something small and smooth. The thing dropped to the floor with a metallic *chink*. It was his mother's ring. The boy picked it up and studied it. Though it had belonged to a homeless woman, the single diamond sparkled radiantly.

Cutting off a length of the thread, he tied the heirloom to the inside of his sack. He stood, took a last, lingering look around the last room his mother had set foot in, and closed the door on that portion of his past.

Moments later his feet were guiding him along the front walk toward the road. The long, lonely path carried him away from the home of his mother's bombast brother. He did not look back.

He was Avery Smith, the boy no one wanted.

Chapter 1
The Rapscallion

Lancashire, England, 8 Years Later

Avery crouched behind a barrel of rotting lettuce heads watching the carriages pass by along the rutted street of Lancashire. Men stood behind their stands in this run-down market place selling all manner of goods. The stench of animals and people was heavy in the air. This was the bad end of town, overrun with peasants and drunkards and thieves. You could not trust half of the men on this block, but then again you most likely could not trust any of the noblemen living in the other end of Lancashire. There were too many people, not enough money, and not near enough food. Most of the people on this street would give their left arm for some decent bread.

Avery, however, was not about to give his left arm for a bite to eat. He tugged at his hood to be sure that it was down over his face. He straightened his legs to stand, but then he held back at the last moment. A little girl had caught his eye. Her face was streaked with dirt and her blond hair was matted into a ragged heap on her small head. The child's mother was close at hand trying to sell rapidly wilting flowers to passers-by. Smith rubbed a hand over his face as he watched her dancing about in the gutter beside one of the vender's carts.

He threw his hood back onto his shoulders and stood up determinedly. Walking casually toward the cart of apples he nodded in greeting to the bearded man behind it.

"Good day to you, sir."

"Good day yourself," the man answered, eyeing Avery's thread-bare clothing suspiciously. "Will you be buying anyfin?"

"I might." Avery leaned on the cart and pointed to the girl. "See that lass yonder?"

The man glanced at the child. "Aye. What of 'er?"

Avery feigned astonishment. "What of her? I understand she's your niece."

The man laughed dryly. "Hehe! She's no niece of mine!"

"Oh no?" Smith rubbed at his chin curiously. "Wha's your name then, good sir?"

"George Mincer."

"Ah, yes! And she's a Mincer same as you!" Avery went on excitedly. "Now I believe it was your…perhaps a brother…what was his name?"

"John?"

"Yes, that's it! That girl there be little Johnette Mincer."

Mincer gawked. "It can't be John!"

"And why not?" Avery lifted one of the apples by the twiggy stem.

"Well-" George spread his big arms wide. "-we're not very close, but I should think he would've told me I had a niece!"

"That's right," Avery answered, rubbing his chin. "He don't live around here anymore, do he? See now," he whispered and both men leaned in close, "I heard that when Mr. Mincer left, his young wife there had to stay here to care for her dying mather. Now that she's passed on Mrs. Mincer can't seem to raise the funds needed to join her dear husband."

George Mincer was now totally fooled by the sly-speaking Avery Smith.

"Now, see Johnette's mather there, George? She sent me over t' ask if the good George Mincer would give an apple to his young niece?"

"Certainly! Certainly! Take it right over!" George shooed Avery away.

"Ah, you're a good man, George. Shall I tell the child who it's from so's she can meet her uncle?" Avery inquired.

George hesitated. "Ah, no. I'll let John make the introductions."

Avery winked. "You've a heart of gold you have, George."

"Good day to you lad! Don't want to keep the lass waiting."

Avery tossed the apple to the little girl as he passed. She caught it and smiled brightly. He simply disappeared around the corner into a dark alley. He pulled the second apple he had palmed from the cart out of his sleeve and bit deeply into the crisp fruit.

Avery Smith sat atop a stable roof by a road on the outskirts of Lancashire in the shade of a towering oak. Avery had long since discovered this as a prime spot for spotting merchants and nobles headed east out of the town.

At age twenty Avery was unemployed, which was the same position he had been in for three years. His wavy brown hair and ragged clothes had odd bits of straw sticking out of them from sleeping in vacant stables and fields. Avery was tall and lanky with clear gray eyes that were constantly studying his surroundings. On his own since the age of twelve, Avery had made a living as a farmhand, store owner's apprentice, and—very briefly—a servant, all in different towns. However, he always ended up returning to his first profession; thievery. In fact, Avery was known throughout Lancashire. He was the dreaded Rapscallion, feared throughout the land, although few had ever seen his face. He was known for approaching his victims with the hood of his cloak down over his lean features and successfully robbing them without ever drawing his weapon; a long dagger which he kept thrust into his belt. He liked to think that the elegant ladies of the King's court dreamed of him as a hero, something like Robin Hood. That the rich gentlemen spoke of him often, ever wary that he might attack their carriages. For it was on these wealthy gentlemen that the Rapscallion preyed.

At long last Avery saw the black smudge of a horse and rider on the road. He crouched behind the peak of the roof to wait until the rider was in plain sight. It was a young man, around twenty-eight or thirty, and Avery could see that he wore fine clothes and rings on his hands. Avery fancied that he heard the jingle of coins as the man passed and headed into the woods at a trot on his high-stepping stallion.

Avery grinned mischievously as he maneuvered his twiggy form down to the ground. Swift and silent, he moved through the woods. Once he was well ahead of the man, he hid beside the road and pulled up the oversized hood on his cloak to bide his time, all the while knowing that one sound could ruin the advantage of surprise. As he watched the man approach, he found himself hoping the encounter did not end in a fist fight. The man was very muscular compared to his own gangling body.

He stepped smoothly out of hiding and caught the horse's bridle. The hood kept his face in shadow but allowed him to see the man's puzzled look.

"Release my animal and let me alone, wretch," he ordered dully.

Avery stroked the horse's muzzle. The large animal snorted and stomped, anxious to be on its way. "This is quite a lovely stallion," he said in a slow, deliberate tone of voice. "He must have cost you a fortune."

"Just what is it that you want?" the man snapped.

Avery held out his hand. "Your purse, m'Lord."

Realization seemed to dawn on the man but rather than turning fearful or angry he seemed smug. "Aahh. I was hoping to run into you, Rapscallion." He let out a long, high whistle.

Four men appeared at both sides of Avery, who grinned and drew his dagger with a flourish. The men brought forth four long fencing sabers. Avery placed the dagger back in his belt with a decisive sigh. Two of the men rushed at him. He jumped back smoothly and ran through the forest. The sounds of his assailants grew closer. They were gaining on him. As he moved, dodging and weaving, he scanned the ground for something to defend himself with. He soon spotted a thick branch just ahead. Dropping into a roll, he grabbed the limb and turned to face his adversaries. The men stopped a few feet away. Two of them brandished their swords and began circling the young thief. They thrust their blades a few times but Avery blocked each attempt.

Suddenly the men lowered their weapons, snickering. Then Avery realized his blunder. In circling with his foes he had placed himself in front of the remaining pair of pursuers. He was surrounded.

Before Avery could turn they had their arms clamped around him. He struggled violently but they managed to drag him back to the road where he stood before his would-be victim of his would-be crime. The man jerked his hood down. He smiled at Avery's frantic expression.

"Wha' do you want?" Smith demanded.

"Your purse, m'Lord."

Avery mustered up the bravado to smile sardonically. "What do you plan to do with me? Do you honestly think I plan to stay captured for very long?"

"Actually, I don't much care what you think or don't think. Your career is at an end, Rapscallion." He spat the word bitterly, as though his mouth were too good to say it. The gentleman leaned in closer. "So tell us, what is your given name?"

The men holding Avery snickered. Avery did not say a word.

The man laughed cruelly and straightened, looming over his captive. "I would advise you not to attempt an escape. Even if you were able to achieve such a thing, we know what you look like now. It wouldn't exactly be difficult to catch you again."

"Methinks the gentleman underestimates me."

The man laughed again. "Just be sure that you don't underestimate *me*," he sneered.

Avery felt the pommel of a sword hilt crash into his skull and watched in horror as his world faded into darkness.

Avery awoke in almost total darkness. His hands were semi-numb due to lack of circulation. With his arms shackled to the wall level with his head, he sat on a thin layer of straw covering a hard layer of stone. He studied his dark cell—for he was in prison—. There were two barred windows, each two feet long and one foot wide; one in the door and one in the wall across from him about six feet up the wall. Other than that, he saw nothing but dark shadows and depressing stones.

This is a fine old predicament, Avery thought to himself as he stared into the night passed the window. *The infamous Rapscallion finally caught.* He snorted bitterly but immediately regretted the action for his head ached like the thunder of a thousand horse hooves. He could no longer feel his fingers when dawn trickled its way into the hazy sky.

The prison seemed to come alive in that instant. He heard a clatter somewhere in the hall and the deep, rasping voices of men. The dim light from the door window strengthened. He heard the key clanking in the lock and the door was flung open a second later. He squinted in the sudden brightness of a flaring torch. A large, lumbering shape entered and thrust a key into his manacles. He felt the cold iron shudder and swing open. He inhaled sharply as he felt the pain in his raw wrists.

The man jerked him roughly to his shaky feet. "Get on," he grunted and thrust Avery out the door.

Avery found himself in a river of prisoners with the current of the crowd pushing him forward. As he walked, Smith rubbed feeling back into his hands painfully. They followed the hall passed many cell doors, and then they were outside in a small square of ground surrounded by an oppressive brick wall. The left side of the ground was taken up by a long table with a bench on both sides. The prisoners mutely sat at the table. Avery pulled his thin cloak closer about him and followed their example. He sat on the end of the bench opposite the wall.

A man with stubby gray hair sat in front of him. "Confounded wobbly seat," he muttered as the wood shook under his weight.

Bowls of what they assumed to be gruel or porridge were placed before them. While the men around him began shoveling the slop into their mouths with their grimy hands, Avery stared down at his own detestable portion.

"You may as well eat up, mate."

Avery looked up and saw the man across the table watching him.

"Tha's all we get 'til sup." The man licked his fingers and raised his eyebrows at young Smith.

Avery shrugged dispiritedly. He scooped up a handful of the mush and slurped it down.

"Well?" the man asked. "How's it taste?"

Avery swallowed thickly and felt the cold gruel slither down his throat. He shuddered. "It doesn't *taste* at all."

"Oh, good," the man joked, "it can't taste bad then, eh?" He laughed at Avery's disgusted face. "Me name's Bruce Portal, but everyone 'ere calls me Porty. An' you'self?"

"Dead where I sit," Avery frowned sardonically.

"Got that right," said a passing guard. "You'll be going t' the gallows a week from tomorrow."

Avery groaned but Porty sighed knowingly. "So you're the one I heard the warden rejoycin' over. The Rapscallion 'as finally been caught."

Avery moaned and put his head in his hand.

Porty's dirt-streaked face turned sympathetic. "Come on, eat up mate."

"What's the point?" Avery shoved the bowl away.

There was the creak of a door opening and then slamming shut. The prisoners went silent and stared. Avery turned and saw an elderly woman, her hair pinned in a tight bun, enter the ground. An old man with a long, white beard stood and followed her through a separate door which Avery had failed to notice. A guard went in after them. The prisoners resumed eating their would-be meal.

"Who was that?" Avery asked Porty.

Porty didn't look up from shoveling in his meal. "Old Mrs. Frattle. She's visited her 'usband every mornin' since he came here."

After the gruel was eaten and the bowls taken up, the men began to walk about the grounds. At six they sat once again at the rickety table to eat their dinner. This time the portions were accompanied by bowls of water but were still cold. At sundown the prisoners filed back into the jailhouse. Avery was padlocked to the wall once again. The door to the cell banged shut and left him alone with his despairing thoughts.

Avery leaned his head back on the stone wall and stared out of the window across from him at the stars. Having spent the day laying on the ground in a half doze, he was in no mood for sleep; however, because he had eaten no more than a mouthful that day, his stomach wouldn't have let him sleep if he had wanted to.

Avery turned his head lazily toward the lock on his cuffs. In a fit of rage he shook his arms, as if he were trying to shake off the metal. He stopped and gulped down a sob of anguish. So this is what it had come to; he had set out to make his life better and was going to die at the gallows as a thief. He ignored the fact that his own greed and pride had brought him to this. Avery tugged at the manacles once more. The dim light from the window reflected off of the pad-lock.

Something happened to Avery at that moment. He resolved not to die, not to remain caged like a wild animal. A plan was already shaping itself in his astute young mind.

Avery sagged down as close to the floor as he could get. After some painful stretching he was able to bring his right foot up to his left wrist and the lock.

Yes, it was feasible. Avery was going to escape.

The next day Avery went out with the rest to the table. He took his seat, picked up his bowl, and began drinking down its contents with a will.

"Well someone's appetite has certainly improved. Wha's gotten into you?" Porty asked with a wry chuckle.

Avery set down his empty bowl and wiped his mouth on the back of his hand. "A new will to live," he grinned.

"Good for you," Porty smirked. "The only problem is that seven days from now you won't *be* alive."

Avery's eyes glinted mischievously as he saw Mrs. Frattle enter the walled square. "We shall see."

While the rest of the men stood idly about, Avery stood against the wall opposite the table. After half an hour, he heard the turning of a knob. Nonchalantly, he began walking toward the door. The guard opened it for Mrs. Frattle and led her to the exit. Just as Avery was about to pass the lady, he tripped on his own shoe. Throwing his arms up he caught her across the neck by accident, and they both fell to the ground in a heap. The guard jerked Avery up only to knock him to the ground again. Mr. Frattle helped his wife to her feet. A thick lock of her gray hair fell over her face.

"I apologize, Ma'am," Avery lamented with his hand on his chin.

The lady snorted her irritation and walked passed him. He watched her saunter away with the guard. He half sat up and felt his mouth with his right hand.

"Wha' happened?" Porty cried as he helped young Smith to his feet.

"I tripped."

"Well you had better watch it next time, mate," Porty sighed. "You're lucky they didn't flog you."

Avery nodded and tried to keep his face solemn. He spent the rest of the afternoon pacing the square yard in silence, putting much effort into keeping his face straight and grave.

At supper he polished off his bowl and waited impatiently for the guards to lead them back to their cells. After what felt like an eternity to Avery, the prisoners were herded back into the jail. Naturally, Avery was pad-locked into his connected shackles on the wall. The guard closed the door behind him. There came the distinct sound of a key turning in the lock. Avery sat still until he was sure the guard was gone.

Slowly, very slowly, he craned his neck up toward his hand. He sat thus for a moment, and, after some swishing around in his mouth, he produced a hairpin through his lips. He had slyly palmed this when he fell with Mrs. Frattle and held it in his cheek. Taking the hairpin in his left hand, he slid downward and brought his leg up until it touched the pad-lock. Avery twisted his foot and turned the keyhole toward him. It was then that he attempted to pick the lock. He watched his hand maneuver the pin seemingly from another world. Sweat beaded upon his brow. Twice he nearly dropped his make-shift tool. His breath caught in his throat.

The lock opened with a soft click, but to Avery it sounded like the slam of a blacksmith's hammer. He stopped dead and waited. No footsteps. No voices.

He dropped the pin and lifted the lock free of the metal loop. The bar swung out on its hinge with a creak. He paused once again but heard only a distant, raspy snoring. He pulled his hands down to his lap, gingerly rubbing his smarting wrists. Young Smith could not help but grin; phase one of his plan had worked.

He stood and shuffled to the door. He peered through the bars in the door and saw a guard sitting at the end of the hall. The man's head was laid back and he was snoring uproariously with an empty bottle hanging loosely in his hand.

Avery breathed a silent sigh and turned back to the cell. Starlight from the window danced on the straw-frosted floor. Now that he was free of the manacles, he must devise a way to escape from the jail itself. He stretched and walked to the window. Looking straight out, he saw a road a few inches below him. The jail was obviously positioned in a small valley beneath the path. He gripped the bars and stared at the moon. Smith soon realized that he wouldn't be able to escape during the day. Nor could he hope to escape through the door at night because of the sentries -the ones that may be awake. The only other way was through the window.

Avery started feeling the bricks and mortar around the bars. Along the top and bottom inside edges of the opening, he discovered a metal strip revealing that the bars were all held together. He also realized that the mortar along the bottom sill was cracked in many places. Just by prying at it with his fingers, he was able to knock a few chunks loose. However, the bars were snugly placed.

He turned and ran his fingers through his hair pensively. Slumped down in the moldy straw, he removed his worn leather shoe. Avery slipped his hand inside it and removed a yellowing handkerchief from within. His outstretched fingers lovingly removed the cloth and caressed his mother's ring. Up until now he had been afraid to look at it. Afraid that someone would attempt to steel it away in the prison yard. Before his capture Avery had gazed upon it almost every night.

He turned the sparkling hoop in his hands and watched the diamond twinkle. He wondered what he would do when he escaped. Presumably he would return to thievery. Granted, he would most likely be forced to travel abroad to elude arrest, but, on the other hand, how many times had he done that before? Yes, Avery's old lifestyle awaited him beyond the dreary, gray stone surrounding him.

He shifted his thoughts to his mother. What would she have wanted for him? Not this. A cold feeling swept over him as he recalled a detail about his mother that he had placed in the back of his mind. No matter how bad things became for them, when he was young, Avery's mother never stole.

And look where it got us, Avery reflected bitterly. *I'm in jail and she*—he didn't let himself finish.

He tucked the cloth-wrapped treasure into his shoe. Avery took one last look at the window and then went to the wall that held his manacles. He took the lock in his left hand and sat stiffly. With his hands placed in the loops, he used his head to push the bar over them. Very carefully, he slipped the lock in place and used his foot to press it shut. Avery then had nothing to do but doze until dawn.

Avery stood against one of the four walls of the yard bumping his head repeatedly against the rock.

Porty made his way toward him. "You'll drive you'self mad doin' that, mate."

"I'm already mad," Avery growled without opening his eyes. He had spent all morning thinking about those bars. There was still no possible way he could think of to escape that way.

Porty chuckled. "'Ow can you go from being so full of hope one day to being so hope*less* the next, eh?"

"It's not that hard, really," Avery muttered.

Porty laughed again and walked away. Avery gazed up at the sky. The clouds were heavy with rain and as gray as his eyes. But no matter how dark the clouds were the sunlight managed to penetrate them that day.

Something dazzled Avery's eyes. He held a hand up to shield them and then looked down to see what it was. Across from him stretched the table and benches. The shining thing was the loose nail in the wobbly seat close to the wall. Avery's eyes lit up with excitement. He hurried to the bench. He could barely keep himself from lunging on it. He straddled the bench with the nail before him. He hunched his back to conceal his movements. Using his nails, he began to pick at the splintery old wood. Chip by chip, piece by piece the wood pulled away from the thick nail. His fingertips became red and sticky. At long last Avery could slip his bloody fingers between it and the board. Slowly, painfully he twisted the nail free. Allowing himself to relax for a moment, he pressed the object in his hands. To anyone else he must have appeared as though he were praying.

The next moment the guard signaled for the men to sit down at the table. Avery slipped the nail into his shoe and swung his leg over the bench to cover the hole. All through dinner he hardly moved; one wrong shake could cause the bench to collapse.

Avery eased the nail free of his shoe later that night. Crouching, he made his way across his cell to the door and peered out the window. His heart plummeted into his stomach.

There was a different guard on duty tonight and this one was dead sober.

Smith ducked below the opening to deliberate with himself concerning his next move. He could wait until the drunkard guard took his watch. But what if that did not occur? There was also the possibility that someone noticed the bloodstains on the wood from his wounded fingertips. Come to think of it, the bench would most likely fall apart tomorrow. There was no way around it. If he was going to escape, it would have to be tonight.

He took another glance at the irritatingly astute man in the hall and turned back to his cell. What could he use? What resources did the cell provide? He noticed a rock in the corner. After a short while a scheme shaped itself in his mind.

The mischievous young Smith snickered as he lifted up the heavy chunk of stone and pressed himself flat against the wall, just out of sight from the door's barred window. Without warning, Avery began screaming at the top of his voice,

"Guard! There's an enormous rat in here! Guard, guard!"

The man groaned. "Oh shut-up!" Footsteps approached and the man kicked roughly at the door.

"I won't!" Avery bellowed back. "Aaahh! Help! Guard!"

Other prisoners began muttering in their own cells. The guard leered angrily through the bars. There came a great gasp when he realized the wall-shackles were empty. "Hoi! Wha's going on here?"

He fumbled with the lock on the door and then flung it open. Avery brought the rock down on the man's head. It hit with a resounding *crack*! The man fell to the floor.

The other inmates' muttering increased. Thinking quickly, he called, "There! That should keep you quiet!"

The whispers died away as Avery slammed the door. He dragged the unconscious man to the shackles. He felt the back of his head to be sure that there was no blood before locking him in place. He ripped two strips of cloth from his cloak and fashioned a gag. As a precaution, he tied the man's ankles to his thighs so he couldn't kick.

With these tasks completed, the desperate young man set to work on the bars. He jammed the point of the nail into a large crack. After some wiggling the point drove through the ancient mortar. Large chunks fell away as he worked. These Avery was careful to catch so they would not crash to the floor. It was sometime after midnight that he finished the top half of the window. In another hour he had most of the bottom edge chipped away. The next time he drove his nail into the stone he felt the bars shift. Avery held his breath. He set down his nail and grasped the bars. He braced himself for the great heave and the clatter that was sure to follow.

He felt rather than heard movements behind him. He turned sharply to see that the guard had come awake and was staring at him, wide-eyed.

In a moment of panic, Avery jerked the bars free and tossed them aside. The crash brought forth a few shouts from the surrounding rooms. He could hear the man struggling behind him. Smith pulled himself up and wriggled through the opening, grasping at the ground before him. He tore violently at the dewy grass.

Then, as quickly as it had begun, it was over. He had pulled himself to freedom. He felt his feet slapping the firm ground. He smelled the foliage and the trees as he veered off the road into the woods. He winced as the rain cascaded down from the sky and began pelting his flushed face.

Avery had escaped the confines of prison, but he had yet to feel the confines of his own repining heart.

Chapter 2
Ms. Manny

Avery gasped for air as he hurtled helter-skelter through the forest. Branches whipped at his face and tore at his clothes. He stumbled as his feet slid in the churned muck of the undergrowth. His whole world was a swirling torrent of rain, thunder, and shadows.

His foot caught on a root and threw him to his knees. He rolled onto his back and could not bring himself to rise. There was a searing ache in his right foot. He wiggled his toes in his left shoe to be sure that the ring was still in place. He sighed and stared up through the rain at the menacing clouds.

He had passed three towns in the four days since the jail break. He had thought of entering each one, but every time there were men on horseback waving a sketch of his likeness in peasants' faces. It had once been impossible to capture the Rapscallion, for none could describe him. Now it was different. Now they had a face to look for.

Avery had been living on berries and stream water, but they never seemed to satisfy his hunger, his thirst. As he lay there in the slushy muck, he could not help but feel that his life had been a waste. He could not even be a thief anymore. He gave into the idea that his life—pitiful before—was now completely ruined.

The clouds broke for a moment overhead and he saw a single, bright star. It was like a beacon to one lost at sea.

His eyelids fell as exhaustion enveloped him.

The next morning Avery felt his energy returning to him quite miraculously. In fact, he felt almost jubilant. Looking back, he soon realized that he never expected to wake from his fitful sleep. He had given up. He laughed out loud and sat up. It was absurd! He was Avery Smith, he never gave up. He determined to continue on and see what became of him.

However, when he got to his feet he discovered a minor setback. A slash the breadth of his palm ran along his right foot. The shoe was cut as well. The gash was not deep, he discovered upon closer inspection, but was enough to cause a limp when he walked. He searched about until he found a long, sturdy branch he could lean on. He then used several roots to bind his slashed shoe to his injured foot. His enthusiasm lessened slightly as he put his foot down gingerly and leaned on the branch.

He hobbled slowly along until he discovered a babbling stream. Smith stopped to quench his thirst. He then removed the improvised bandage and washed the congealed blood from the wound. Avery was just rebinding the cut when he heard a horse neighing in the distance. He sat frozen for a moment and then peered through the thick brush behind him.

Avery caught sight of a rundown cottage nestled within a small clearing before him. The two porch steps had rotted and caved in. The porch roof was practically nonexistent for the holes. The shutters were nailed in place over the windows. Beside the cottage was a decrepit barn covered with peeling white paint. Grazing peacefully behind the house was a young stallion with a shadowy brown coat. His tail and mane were midnight black. Avery noticed that there was a white star shaped spot between the animal's eyes.

He took one last cautious glance around before venturing forth into the yard. The horse turned and snorted in his direction. He rubbed the stallion's muzzle to calm him. After the horse had returned to his grass and was nonchalantly chomping away, Avery made his way to the house. He peered through a small gap in the boards, but he stared in vain for the inside of the cottage was concealed in shadows. Slowly, he limped his way to the door. After jiggling the handle, the creaking door shoved inward.

"Who's there?" a hoarse voice demanded loudly.

Avery jumped in spite of himself and had to grab the door frame to keep from losing his balance.

"Speak up!" the voice rasped. Shuffling was heard from within and the rasping apparition stepped into the light. Avery had to hold his breath to keep from laughing aloud.

An old woman with wild hair and a crumpled dress wielding a large rolling pin stepped forward. "Hm!" she grunted and jabbed the rolling pin at the air. "Be ye man or beast?"

"Um, hello," Avery mumbled as his astonishment receded. The woman turned sharply in his direction.

She poked him hard in the chest with her pin. "Who are ye?"

"I am-"

"Shut-up!" she spat. "What do ye want wi' me?"

"I-"

"Why did ye come here?" She waved the wooden pin at Avery menacingly.

"Well I—I thought this house was abandoned."

"Well it's not!"

"Clearly," Avery commented mildly and turned away, his cane making a dull *thunk* on the rotten floorboards as he went. He had just stepped off of the porch when the woman spoke again, softer this time.

"Wait…wait," she called. Her withered hands felt the air before her. It was at that moment Avery realized why the woman had not hit him over the head on sight. It was because she did not have the gift of sight; she was blind.

"Was…was there something ye needed?"

Avery limped forward and held his arm out for her to feel. "You look like you could use more help then me, ma'am."

She prodded his arm with her rolling pin and glared in his direction. "Don't ye underestimate me, my lad." They paused for a moment and she seemed to study him with her mind. "Wha's yer name?"

"Avery."

As soon as he said this, Avery wondered if he should have presented a false name. He decided on the negative. The men looking for him had only a vague sketch and this lady had only a name.

"I'm Miss Mary May Jamerson," she declared. "But ye may call me Ms. Manny."

Avery smiled to himself. Ms. Manny was a bitter old hag, but she seemed sensible.

"Now, if ye are able to keep a civil tongue in your head, I'll allow ye to share my dinner wi' me."

Avery stepped in after her and stared around. All of the walls were hidden behind tall shelves. A large variety of objects were scattered about these shelves; some held one thing while others held twenty. In one corner was a small bed piled high with quilts beside a fireplace. The only light in the one-room cottage was a shutter-less window above a small table. Avery watched Ms. Manny make her way to the shelf beside this table. She set her rolling pin on its shelf and placed a loaf of bread and a jar of honey on the table.

"Come, come," Ms. Manny offered with a wave of her crinkly hand.

Avery sat in one of the two chairs, ripped off a portion of the bread, and began devouring it ravenously. He paused long enough to drizzle some honey on the remainder of his helping.

"Don't they feed ye where ye come from?" she inquired with an upraised eyebrow.

"Let's just say that I've been down on me luck," Avery replied in a weary voice with a rye smile.

Ms. Manny nodded. "Are ye a cripple?" she asked suddenly.

"Hardly." He felt a sting of offense at the remark.

"Then why do ye use a cane? And don't look so astonished. Me eyes may be useless but ma hearing still works."

"I cut me foot last night," Avery explained.

Ms. Manny nodded. "If ye look on the shelf beside me hearth ye'll find some clean linen."

Smith retrieved the thin material and began wrapping his foot.

"Where do ye live, Avery?"

He snorted acridly. "Nowhere at the moment." Ms. Manny's face turned thoughtful and before he could stop himself Avery confessed, "To be quite honest Ms. Manny, I was recently…liberated from prison."

"Ah," she murmured. "And what were you imprisoned for?"

Avery felt pinned down by those sightless, milky eyes that blazed in his direction.

"Mistakes which I hope never to repeat again," he answered simply.

"Right," Ms. Manny said to herself with finality. "Listen to me lad, seems to me like ye could use as much help as I could. So, if ye're willing to help me around the house and run errands to the market, I'll allow ye to share ma food and stay in ma barn. What say ye?"

"I say you're offering me a job as a housekeeper."

Ms. Manny pointed an accusing finger at him. "Ye don't have to accept it ye know! I'll admit it's not the best situation in the world but it's all I've got to give ye!"

"I'm sorry," Avery insisted hastily. "I didn't mean to insult you. I'd be happy to stay here."

Ms. Manny straightened and put on a noble air. "Ye just mind that ye keep those thoughts in ye head, ungrateful whelp."

"Yes, Ms. Manny," Avery smiled.

"Now clear the table. The food goes on the second shelf down behind me," she ordered. Avery chuckled quietly at the lady's officious manner. "Ye'll soon learn," she went on, "that I keep everything in a certain place. I went blind a year ago January and it took me months to get this system worked out."

"Yes, Ms. Manny."

Avery awoke the next morning buried in a mound of hay. He sat up and brushed bits of hay from his clothes before making the short trek to the house. Ms. Manny was waiting for him at the rickety table. "In yer opinion young Avery, what needs to be done around ma house?"

Avery ceased shoveling bread into his mouth and thought. "The porch steps need to be rebuilt, the leg on this table needs to be fixed, and you could use some firewood-"

"And A need ye to go to the market this afternoon. A'd go with you but me old bones just don't move as well as they used to."

Avery let out a weary breath. "That's a lot to cover."

Ms. Manny stood up and made her way across the room. "A didn't say you had to do it all today. Now, A'll be needing some cream, eggs, and bread." She lifted a purse onto the table from her pocket and removed three coins. "Ye may buy yourself a little something as well."

"All righ'."

Avery reached for the coins but Ms. Manny covered them with her hand.

"A'm allowing ye to stay, Avery," she whispered in her harsh voice, "but A'm still not sure if A trust ye. Do ye have anything of value?"

"What?"

Ms. Manny sighed impatiently. "Insurance. Did ye think I would let ye walk away wit' me money on trust that A haven't given ye?"

"I guess not," Avery murmured irritably and ran his fingers through his dark hair. Reluctantly, he removed his untorn shoe and took out the ring that he so cherished. "Here," he mumbled sternly and thrust the golden circle at the old woman. "My mother's ring." He knew this was a smart move for Ms. Manny to make, but he did not like it.

She took the ring and felt it in her hands. Her thumbnail tapped at the diamond. "Right. On your way then."

"Before I go," Avery began, "may I borrow a needle and thread? Me shoe is in need of repair."

Ms. Manny pointed out the shelf containing these materials as she cleared the table.

"Have ye no weapon, Avery?" she inquired suddenly as he sat stitching the soft leather shoe.

He looked at her strangely. "I had a blade, but they took it at the jail."

"Ye'll need one in the market." He stared at her. She seemed to feel his eyes and sense the question within them. "As a precaution, of course."

"Me staff will suffice." He bent over his work once more.

Ms. Manny tilted her head and Avery once again had the feeling that he was being studied by those creamy eyes. "Ye *are* a resourceful one aren't ye? I reckon ye've had a hard time of it in life, though ye're young."

"Yes, Ms. Manny," Avery breathed.

Avery split numerous logs for Ms. Manny's fire before setting out toward the market. It wasn't until Ms. Manny offered him an oversized, hooded cloak to ward off the fall winds that Avery realized that he might be recognized in the small bazaar. His past had always followed him before, and he had no reason to believe that it would not follow him thus far. He so regretted all of the things he had stolen, the choices he had made. In jail, while he was planning to escape, all he had wanted was to come back to his old life; his thievery. Now he wanted more than that. When Avery had left his uncle's home and gone into the world, he had buried his desire to be better deep within himself, just under the need to survive. That desire, which was so long forgotten, that echo of the boy he once was, was now stirring inside him again. It was like an old wound that was slowly opening once more. With it came a profound hopelessness. Avery had ruined his life and he felt he could never repair it. He would have to go through life covering his face; hiding in the shadows of shame. He could not afford to be recognized.

"Ms. Manny," he called urgently, "I need something to cover my face!"

She frowned. "What for?"

His quick mind formulated a lie. "I-I have burns, on me face."

The old woman straightened and reached toward him. "Let me feel."

"No!" Avery said too quickly. "I don't want you to picture it; nor do I want anyone else to see it," he finished lamely. He did not like to lie to the old woman, but neither could he betray her trust.

"Oh," Ms. Manny huffed. "See what ye can find."

After some rummaging about, he came across the roll of linen which he had used to wrap his foot. Avery carefully tied the gauzy cloth over his eyes and nose so that he could still see enough to walk about.

Staff in hand and coins in his pocket, Avery departed for the market. It was less than a mile up the dusty road and surrounded by a cluster of houses and wide fields beyond. He passed only one building, which had a sign indicating a physician, before he came to the small market.

The wide streets were a swirling mass of people, noise, and dust. Avery tapped the path before him and did his best to feign blindness, for that was his chosen excuse if anyone inquired as to his bandage. *Perhaps this should be my profession in the future,* he mused to himself, *Disguises and intrigue.*

Avery moved up one street and down another while day dreaming of spying and selling secrets for great profit. He made his way through alleys and crisscrossed the square but to no avail. On one street they sold fabrics, on another beads and pretty ornaments, but no one seemed to be selling food.

"Are ye lost good sair?" The kindly voice cut through the noise of the crowd.

Through the hazy wrap about his face Avery saw that a young woman was addressing him. He could not see her face very well, but her voice sounded young and carried a thick accent.

"Yes, fair lady," Avery replied quietly.

"Then, if et pleases ye, A'll be leading ye through here." She placed a delicate hand on his arm. "Where is et ye need to be going?"

"I need to find the food vendors, maiden."

The woman steered him around the square to a side road. Avery faintly smelt lavender mingled with bread and spices. He could hear the peddlers shouting their wares.

"Shall A gather ye purchases, sair?" the girl asked sweetly and pressed his arm with her dainty hand.

"Nay good lady," Avery smiled, "my nose shall lead me from here. You have placed me on my path."

She giggled merrily. "Good day to ye, sair." She bobbed a curtsy and was gone as quickly as she had appeared.

Avery procured Ms. Manny's things and some salted ham for himself. He was tempted to buy a tankard of ale as well but thought better of it. Once this was finished he threaded his way through the town and walked back to Ms. Manny's cottage. Smith set the parcels on the table and turned to Ms. Manny. She was sitting on her bed with her hand on her chest. Her breath came in heavy gasps and seemed to be painful.

"Ms. Manny?" Avery spoke tentatively. He slipped a long fingertip under the edge of the gauze and slid it off of his face.

"Water," she gasped out.

Avery turned full circle in the room before asking, "Where? From where?"

"There." The old woman pointed to the floor beside the table.

For the first time, Avery noticed the trap door. He flung it open and descended down the stairs revealed within. There he discovered a well and a meager store of food. He ladled out some water and rushed it up to the lady. After Ms. Manny had sipped at the water her breathing seemed to become calmer.

"Thank ye, lad."

Avery took the ladle from her as he knelt beside the bed. "Are you alrigh'?"

Ms. Manny laughed slightly. "A'm *old.*"

He nodded and paused before speaking. "Why didn't you tell me about the…cellar before?"

She leaned toward him. "I didn't trust you."

"And now?"

Ms. Manny held out her wrinkled hand. "Where's me change?" Avery dropped the coins into her hand. Ms. Manny felt the dull money with her fingertips. "We'll see."

Avery grinned. "Yes, Ms. Manny."

Thief of the Gallows

Spring melted slowly into summer as Ms. Manny's health melted slowly away. By August she was practically bedridden and Avery had taken to sleeping on the floor before the hearth incase she needed something in the night. She had become like a grandmother to him, even though he hardly felt this attachment.

After two months of sleeping in her barn and running her errands, Avery had mastered her 'system' of giving everything a place. In that time he had repaired her roof and the steps of her porch and anything else he found in disarray. All the while his worry for his aged companion grew.

One morning, as Avery was searching for more toils to fill his day, someone knocked at the door. This was something that had not happened since Avery had arrived himself.

"Who is it?" Ms. Manny croaked from her bed.

The man answered although he could not possibly have heard her.

"A constable of Lancashire, mum."

The word seemed to freeze Avery's very soul; *Lancashire*. His voice became a mere lump in his throat and plummeted to the bottom of his stomach. His muscles refused to move and he stood staring all around the room as if silently begging for help from the furniture. Finally his ears began to work again and he heard the pounding on the door and Ms. Manny's order for him to answer it. Avery snatched up the gauze mask and called, "A moment!" as he positioned it on his face. "A moment!" He threw the cloak over his shoulders and yanked the hood down to cover his forehead.

Avery opened the door with shaking hands and sweating palms. He worked hard to keep his breathing normal as he stammered "G-good day sir." Despite his best efforts, he could not keep a stutter from his speech.

"Good day," the constable said almost matter-of-factly. "I have been sent out to track down an escaped prisoner from the Lancashire prison." The man held up a sheet of parchment with Avery's likeness inked upon it.

"Why have you ventured so far for this fugitive? Is he some murderer?" Avery asked softly in an attempt to disguise his voice.

"Not at all," he said with a heavy sigh. "However, my superiors have been chasing this one for sometime. He is a thief, you see, by the name of Rapscallion and the blaggard has quite a reputation. The peasants say that he has no face and that he can disappear into thin air."

Avery took a bitter pleasure in the knowledge that his reputation had grown larger than he thought.

"It's all utter rubbish of course. He escaped after just three days in jail. So you see why the warden is angry," the man concluded wearily. "Claims it was a *lack of proper security*," he mocked.

"Ah," Avery tried to force himself to breathe. "Well, as much as I would like to, I'm afraid I can't help you. This bandage impairs me vision somewhat." Avery touched the wrap lightly as he spoke.

"And your companion there?" The constable nodded over Avery's shoulder at Ms. Manny.

"She is completely blind, sir."

"I see." The man's features visibly sagged. "I shall be in town for a day or two in the event that you see something." He mounted his horse and trudged away.

Avery exhaled heavily as he shut the door. He felt the ice that had formed in his blood transform into the feverish perspiration of fear. Avery wondered briefly if the man had been an apparition projected by his mind; that he was going mad and beginning to hallucinate. But Avery knew that the meeting had been no vision. He felt that his time with Ms. Manny, though short-lived, was almost at its end.

Chapter 3
On the Road Again

Avery slept lightly before the smoldering fire and tossed on the wood floor. He had many dreams of his mother that night. He would be walking toward her, but she would push him away; or she would be sitting high above him and he could not reach her. In the last of these nightmares, there was a strong wind blowing toward him and whenever he would take a step closer to his mother it would drive him back with vehement gusts. Avery awoke with a start, still hearing what he thought to be the blowing of imaginary wind. He sat up and saw Ms. Manny struggling for breath and drenched in sweat.

Avery stumbled to his feet and leaned over his old companion. "Ms. Manny? Ms. Manny!" He spoke in restrained urgency.

"G…get…Bellings…" she gasped in her hoarse voice. "Doc…tor…"

Avery placed his hand on the lady's silvery hair. "I will," he breathed in earnest. "I'll get the doctor."

He leapt nimbly to his feet and rushed out the back door. As he ran to the barn he felt the night breeze whipping his billowy shirt about. Avery flung open the barn door and the gate of the lone horse's cell. The stallion, whose name was Pinpoint, neighed at him reluctantly. Avery jumped onto his back without bothering to remove the animal's blanket and dug his heels into the poor beast's sides. Pinpoint shot out of the barn and blazed along the dark road with Avery clinging to his flowing mane. They flew down the path with the dew falling upon them. A distinct chill was in the air. Avery's teeth chattered and rattled in his head. He halted the horse before the modest building and sprang to the damp ground. He pounded his fist upon the door.

"Dr. Bellings! Dr. Bellings!"

"What?" The door was flung open by a man slightly older than Avery wearing a nightshirt and pants. He had a flannel nightcap atop his head which shook whenever he spoke. "What is happening?" he added more gently at the sight of Avery's desperate face.

"It's Ms. Manny! You must come!"

"Wait here." The man shut the door for a brief moment and emerged fully dressed with a bag in his hand. "I must fetch my horse," he sighed.

"Take mine," Avery ordered.

"I'll be needing a saddle."

Avery, quite frustrated by these delays, ran to the man's barn and retrieved the saddle. Together they strapped it onto Pinpoint's strong back. Just as Dr. Bellings mounted, Avery slapped Pinpoint's flank and he shot off into the night. Avery paused to watch them fade from sight before going to the barn once again. He saddled the doctor's own horse and positioned the bridal. He did not make the animal run, but rather let him choose his own speed. Now that the doctor was on his way there was no hurry. Avery held the horse back at times but would not admit the reason to himself. *I don't want to wear out another man's ride*, he told himself.

Avery dismounted before the front steps and left Dr. Belling's animal beside Pinpoint. He saw the flickering of candlelight through the cracks in the shutters. Taking a long breath, Avery forced himself to open the door. It swung inward and he stood in the threshold staring.

Dr. Bellings was sitting on the far side of Ms. Manny's bed holding her hand. His bag lay on the table with odd looking instruments scattered about it. Ms. Manny's breathing was still coming in ragged gasps. Avery stepped forward and the doctor looked up. His brow was darkened by a frown and his eyes were hazy.

In that moment, Avery knew what was to come.

He could hold back no longer. Avery ran to his companion's side as the doctor stepped away from the bed. "Ms. Manny?" he whispered.

"Ye…ye're late…lad," she choked.

Avery smiled weakly and took her feeble hand in his own.

"Ms. Manny," he began, "I lied to you. See?" He pressed her hand to his cheek and heard her emit a small cry through the wheezing. "No burns."

Ms. Manny grinned and seemed to be laughing. "I knew ye was." this statement was followed by a bout of coughing. "Can ye...read...Avery?"

"Yes." Avery's entire body was trembling despite his efforts to stop it.

Ms. Manny reached under her pillow and handed Avery a small black book. "Fly away...Avery," she murmured. "Fly away."

The room seemed to darken and all three were silent. The candles flickered dimly. Ms. Manny's hand felt cold and still in Avery's own.

Avery felt as though his heart had stopped along with Ms. Manny's. He stood up and backed into the table. He slipped the black book into his pocket numbly and watched Dr. Bellings check for a pulse in his companion, his friend.

"I'm sorry," he shook his head.

"Me too," Avery choked.

"I know it wasn't your fault lad, but-"

Avery turned sharply to look the man in the eye. "But what?" Somehow he did not need to ask.

"I recognize you," he answered simply, "from the drawing." Dr. Bellings shrugged half sympathetically, but there was a stern glint in his eye. "I have to turn you in."

Avery's thieving instincts came alive as his brain issued one command; *run*. He turned and raced out of the cabin. He leapt onto Pinpoint and slapped his flank with all his might. Avery gripped his mane and leaned forward as the stallion reared up and neighed at the sky. Pinpoint sped down the road at a breathtaking pace. Avery turned and saw Bellings rush out the door and stand on the road watching him. After he lost sight of the house Avery looked ahead and saw the small market and Bellings's office looming up before him. Dawn was slithering into the clouded sky just as Avery stopped in the square. All was silent.

"There!"

The shout rang through the air and Avery looked around to find the source. It was the constable from Lancashire emerging from an alley on his left.

"Stop him!" This came from the doctor, who rode into the square behind Avery.

Avery spun Pinpoint to the right and cantered out of town and up a nearby hill. He looked over his shoulder once as he crested the rise. The constable had a crossbow pointed at Avery's chest. Avery dipped out of sight just as the constable released his arrow. At the bottom of the hill was a small wooded valley. Avery could hear his pursuers galloping behind him. He felt the thud of Pinpoint's hooves beating in time with his heart. He looked over his shoulder once more just as the constable pulled another arrow from the quiver fastened to his saddle. Avery spun abruptly left, weaving haphazardly through the trees. A low stone wall appeared ahead.

Pinpoint leapt over the wall and Avery expected him to land immediately; however, once they were over the wall, there was nothing but space beneath them. Avery looked down and realized that there was no ground for at least seven feet. They seemed to be flying over a dried up river bed. Avery's mouth opened in a silent scream.

Pinpoint's front hooves landed securely—mercifully—on solid ground while his back hooves landed on the very edge of the bank and slipped back. The capable stallion regained his balance and galloped away into the woods propelled by sheer panic. The constable and Bellings halted just short of the stone wall with their steeds chomping irritably at their bits. The constable fired a last weary shot at Avery. The man's shaking hands caused the missile to fly far to Avery's left.

Avery had once again outrun his past.

Thud! Thud!

Avery pounded on the heavy wooden door with his fist. He let out a steamy breath and wiped the rain from his eyes as he waited for an answer. Pinpoint's blanket was wrapped around his shoulders and over his head where the rain had plastered it to his forehead. Pinpoint stood behind him nudging at his shoulder with his muzzle.

The door creaked half way open and a large man poked his head out. "Wot is it?" he demanded squinting into the moonlight through the downpour.

"I wondered if I might do some work for you in exchange for a room for the night."

"Don take charity," he grunted, "much less give et."

He started to close the door but Avery blocked it with his foot.

"Sir," he pleaded, "I haven't eaten in three days." He contorted his face into what he fervently hoped was a desperate look.

"Marty?" A woman's voice rang out from somewhere within the tavern. "'ho is it?" A plump woman appeared beside the man called Marty. Blond ringlets adorned her round head and her cheeks were tinged with rouge.

"Ah, no one, moi love," Marty insisted. "He was just leavin'." He tried to press the door shut, but his wife took hold of the handle.

"What was it yar needing then, lad?"

"Nothing!" Marty put in.

The lady rolled her eyes. "Come in, lad. Wee'll let you work a bit, and stay the night if ya like. We need the help at the moment."

The man groaned. "Oh fine! If ya can clear the tables and wash the dishes then ya got a bed for the night and break'ast in the mornin'." He glared at his wife who answered with batted lashes and a wide smile.

Avery grinned and his shoulders sagged with relief. "Thank you, sir." He stabled Pinpoint and hurried into the kitchen of the secluded inn.

He spent two uneventful hours bussing tables. At ten o'clock three men entered and sat at a corner booth. Avery noticed a young boy standing close by them and soon realized that this bedraggled lad was the butt of numerous jests from the men. The boy stood with his eyes downcast, making no motion to defend himself.

After glancing to be sure that neither the round owner, nor his wife, were watching, Avery made his way over to the men.

"Hello there!" he exclaimed cheerfully. He balanced the crate of dirty dishes that he had been collecting on his hip and half grinned at the rough looking men. "Is this boy bothering you, gents?"

The men scowled at Avery suspiciously. "Wot makes yew say tha'?" asked one particularly dirty man with a long, greasy black beard.

"Just noticin'," Avery spoke coolly and tried to match their speech so as to put them at ease, "that you three seem ta be pickin' on 'im a lot."

"Yeah," leered a gray haired man. "He's our property to do wif as we loikes."

"Oh, I see." Avery turned to look at the lad. He raised his eyes curiously and Avery winked at him. "An' how does three gents as you come by such a littol servant as this?"

The third man half rose. "He wos owed us!" The other two nodded emphatically.

"Owed to you?" Avery was taken aback. "He's a person!"

Black beard snorted, "He's payment. His father owed us some money but 'e wouldn't pay up." He jerked his greasy head at the lad. "So we took 'im instead. Ain't that rioght, Creeny?"

The man with ragged red hair smirked wickedly and nodded. "Rioght, Sal."

The one called Sal turned back to Avery, "Now on yor way!" He took a long draft from his tankard.

The man with gray hair took some dice from his pocket. "We got things ta do."

But Avery would not, for the dice had caused a spark in his mind. "How's about a littol gamble?" Avery stepped forward, tripped on his own shoe, and caught the table to regain his balance. The decrepit table shook violently and the dice clattered to the floor. "Oops. I got et." Avery set his crate on the ground and stooped to retrieve the dice.

"Hey, Smith!" Avery looked up and saw the round man calling to him from the bar. "Back t' the kitchen wi' ye!"

"'Scuse me," Avery said to the men as he straightened. He took the crate to the kitchen and deposited the dishes into the tub of soapy water. He then began looking frantically about the cramped room. He soon spotted a jar of tacks alongside some other tools on a shelf above the washtub.

"Smith, wot's keeping ye?" the round man called.

The tacks, Avery decided, would be perfect for the part. He snatched two from the jar and made his way back to the dinning room where he cleared some dishes before approaching the three again.

"So, how 'bout et?"

The man with gray hair glared. "Wot?"

"A gamble," Avery grinned amiably. "We roll the dice. If I win I get the boy."

Sal eyed him irritably. "An' wot are *yew* gonna bet?"

Avery pretended to consider for a moment. "My horse."

Creeny nodded. "Rioght. Soon as the whelp finds me dice we'll play."

Avery knelt out of sight and saw the boy fumbling below the table. Avery produced the dice from his sleeve and smiled at the dumbfounded boy. They straightened in unison.

"Here they are," Avery said and set the dice on the table. "Gentleman first, eh?"

The men laughed and Sal took the dice. He shook them about for a time and then let them fall. The dice rolled, clattered against a tankard, and landed flat; a five and a three.

"That's, erm...eight, lads! Ha ha!" Sal and his cronies sniggered and smirked at the boy. "Yor turn now," he sneered at Avery.

Avery put on a grave face and took up the dice in his hands. He closed his eyes and fiddled about with them in his fists as though he were praying. In reality, he was pressing the tacks into the wooden dice on the sides opposite the sixes. Avery's eyes flickered open and he let the dice fall. They rolled for a moment and the boy tensed at his side. The two cubes teetered on a corner and then fell still. The men gasped and Sal's eyes grew wide with surprise.

"Huh," Avery snorted. "I won." The boy stared in shock at the dice. Avery picked up the wooden squares and fiddled with them again, as if making sure that every side didn't have a six. "Well I must say, you gents came out better than I," Avery explained in mock forlornness, "I've been trying to get rid of that horse for years." He lifted the crate and turned to the bar with the boy close behind.

"Oh sir-"

"Wait," Avery ordered quietly. He inquired of the man, "Have I done enough for a bite to eat rather than bed and breakfast, sir?" The round man grunted and handed him two biscuits with some salted ham in the middle of each. He thanked him and led the boy to the barn.

"Sir!" the boy beamed up at Avery. "Thank you! Those men took me a month ago yesterday."

"Really?" Avery mused pensively as he lifted a bridle from a peg on the wall. "Is it true then about your father's debts?" He strapped the harness on Pinpoint, who was standing quite still.

The boy shrugged. "My father hired them last summer to help build our new barn. They always complained that he hadn't paid them enough."

Avery swung onto Pinpoint's back and extended his hand to help the boy into the saddle behind him. "What's your name?"

"Todd Genellsteen, sir."

"And where is home for you Todd Genellsteen?" Avery grinned.

Todd pointed down the road. "Away westward, sir."

Avery clucked to his horse and urged him forward at a trot. They rode all night and Avery felt Todd's head against his back. His even breaths assured him that the boy slumbered. Avery shook him awake an hour before dawn for directions and by the time the sun rose they had stopped before a small farmhouse. Todd sat in a state of ecstasy staring at the house. The door opened and a tall man with black and gray speckled hair stepped out.

"Todd?" he called.

Todd leapt from the saddle and ran to meet him. Avery allowed them a moment's private embrace before dismounting himself.

"Ah!" Mr. Genellsteen rushed to Avery and shook his hand vigorously. "Thank you good sir! You have restored my very life!" Avery could not help but smile at these praises. "Please," Mr. Genellsteen went on, "is there anything I can do for you in return?"

"Well," Avery began sheepishly, "I haven't had a full meal in days."

"Say no more!" the man laughed joyously. "Our home is your home!"

The generous Genellsteens fed Avery a dinner of meatpies and buttered bread. Pinpoint dined on oats and grass. They then presented him with a warm cloak and provisions for five days at the very least.

Avery turned Pinpoint to the northwest and once again began chasing the horizon.

Chapter 4
The Fishing Boat

Avery walked Pinpoint down a small hill and stopped on the sandy bank of a bubbling stream. Pinpoint buried his nose in a tuft of grass and began munching away. Avery removed a meatpie and a flask of wine from his saddlebag and plopped down to eat it. He sipped at the wine and stared forlornly at the rambling water before him.

His thoughts turned to Ms. Manny. How he mourned his old companion! Avery recalled the small black book which she had presented to him with her dying breath. Up until now he had been too distraught to look at it; the memories were too fresh. But, now that his curiosity was agitated, he couldn't help but pull it out of his pocket.

Stamped on the binding in gold lettering was the title of the thick book. Bible. On the cover in the same gold print was the name Mary May Jamerson. The Bible was very old and worn. Avery feared the leather binding would fall apart when he opened it. He carefully lifted the cover of the ancient book and flipped through the yellowing pages.

It was like trying to read Greek. It was not that Avery could not read, it was simply that the way this book was worded confused him. He could not make head nor tales of it. *What do I need with books anyway?* Avery thought solemnly. He slipped the book back into his pocket to keep as a memento of his deceased friend.

Pinpoint snorted and pushed at Avery's cheek with his muzzle. "Yeah, yeah," Avery murmured as he stood up. He pulled an apple from the saddlebag and fed it to his large beast.

Click.

Avery straightened quickly with his eyes wide. He glanced around and heard the cooing of a small animal. He relaxed and settled down to sleep.

Avery's eyes snapped open and his heart quickened. He tried to stand but there was a great weight on his back and arms. He opened his mouth to shout and a loathsome smelling gag was immediately tied in place. Ropes began cutting into Avery's wrists and ankles as the weight lifted from his back. Two pairs of hands roughly forced him to roll over so that he was looking skyward. Three grizzly faces leaned over him, each with a smirk plastered below his nose. Avery stared in horror at the three men from the inn the day before.

"Well, well," snickered Sal, "wot have we got 'ere?"

"A liddle street rat," spat the gray haired man with an almost toothless grin.

The other two cackled savagely. The boot of Creeny collided with Avery's right temple and his world slipped into darkness.

Swish. Swish.

Avery's ears perceived the splash and trickle of waves while the briny sent of seawater distracted his nostrils. His stomach lurched with nausea from the motions of the floor beneath him. He forced himself to open his eyes and look around. He was on a boat, locked in a dim store-room and surrounded by crates. The offensive gag had been removed but his feet and hands were still bound. The back of his head throbbed, but he could not muster up the energy to feel for the lump that must have appeared there. A small lump in the toe of his shoe let him know that his mother's ring was still with him, which seemed to be a comfort in some small way. Avery also felt the weight of Ms. Manny's Bible in his pocket. By twisting about and lifting himself onto one elbow, he was able to reach a sitting position against the wall. He instantly regretted this, for it made his head hurt all the more. His muscles refused to cooperate, so he lay back and tried to ignore his slight sea-sickness.

The ancient door opposite of him creaked open on its rusty hinges. Creeny, the youngest man in the group of captors, stepped in and deposited another box in the corner.

"Where are we bound?" Avery inquired of him with a voice hoarse with thirst.

The man turned with a sound somewhere between a grunt and a snicker. "Ireland," he answered. "An' when we gits there, we gonna sell ye to a merchant friend of ours." He slammed the door and left young Smith to ponder his misfortune.

No you won't! Avery thought to himself. The light of determination sparked in his eyes and flowed through his veins. He had let himself give up once and he had sworn to never do it again. *If I can escape from the Lancashire jail,* Avery told himself, *then surely I can escape these half-wits!*

Avery sat with his back to a wooden box. He grunted in pain as his nimble fingers dug at the wood around the head of a nail. He stopped abruptly as footsteps sounded above him. He strained to listen over the beat of his own heart.

"Whin do ye fink we'll reach the port?"

A second voice answered, "'bout five 'hours past noontide."

Avery wasted no more time listening and immediately began digging for the nail. He groaned as his fingertips were ripped to shreds by splinters of wood. After an hour of painful scratching, he pulled the nail free. Without delay, he began picking at the rope that held him with the point of the freed nail.

Sooner than Avery wished—for he was only halfway through the rope—the door opened. He slipped the nail into his cuff as Creeny and Sal stepped in. Both were wearing wicked grins on their faces. Without a word they jerked him to his feet and led him out the door. On deck the failing light dazzled Avery's eyes. He realized that the vessel was not a ship but a small fishing boat. They led him to the end of the gangplank where Avery caught sight of Pinpoint. The older man held Pinpoint's reins and was chatting to a man Avery had never seen before. He wore a velvet coat and trousers with a stiff ruff at his throat.

"A'll give ye thirty shillins for t'e boy and t'e brute," the man said in a thick Irish drawl. He gestured vaguely at the irritable Pinpoint.

"Thirty?!" the gray haired man cried in outrage. "They're worth at least fifty!" he snapped.

The other two rushed in behind him with more vehement protests. Avery was left standing behind them; unsupervised. He began wrestling with the half severed rope as the men haggled loudly.

"Fifty!"

"Thirty."

"Forty!"

"Thirty."

"Thirty-five!"

"Thirty."

The rope fell to the ground along with the nail. He leapt onto Pinpoint's back.

"Done."

"*No!*" the merchant shouted. "Get 'im lads!"

Avery heard their shouts waning into the distance as he spurred Pinpoint onward to their unknown fate along the road.

Chapter 5
Tom and Gilbert Haddley

Avery trudged through the wide field with Pinpoint beside him. After escaping he had ridden all night and most of the next day without passing a town. He had slipped into a dreary sleep that afternoon and awakened at dawn the next morning only to tramp onward without purpose.

Pinpoint bit and chomped at tufts of grass as they walked.

"It's much easier for you," Avery grumbled moodily. "You can find breakfast anywhere. You're lucky I haven't cooked *you* for dinner." Pinpoint snorted doubtfully.

Suddenly the animal's ears perked and he hurried forward. "Where are you off to?" Avery called after him.

Pinpoint only trotted faster. Snatching at the reins, Avery looked ahead and saw the back of a small farmhouse before them. With a sudden burst of energy he ran toward it.

Beside the barn he spotted a large watering trough where Pinpoint stood drinking his fill. Avery fell to his knees beside it and submerged his whole face into the clear water. He sat back and let the November wind blow over his sopping face and neck. He shivered involuntarily.

Unknown to Avery, the door of the cabin opened and a man of his own age stepped out. "Sair?"

Smith tried to jump to his feet but stumbled backward on the edge of his cloak and collapsed in a crumpled heap, enveloped by his exhaustion.

Avery gasped as he awoke to a foul smelling liquid beneath his nostrils. He squeezed his eyes shut and shoved the bottle—which was emitting the obnoxious fumes—away from his face.

"A think 'e's coming around."

"'e looks harf drunk."

Avery opened his eyes and saw two blurry shapes leaning over him and whispering among themselves.

"Ye'd look drunk too if ye had this stuff stuck in yor face, Gilly." The shadowy shape took the bottle and set it aside.

Avery blinked and rubbed his eyes. When he lifted his eyelids he saw two men sitting beside him. One had sandy blond hair and looked to be about thirty years old. He stroked a stubby beard while his skeptical brown eyes studied Avery. The other looked to be Smith's own age with black hair and sparkling green eyes. Although he was young, there were several early wrinkles around his mouth as a result of smiling.

Avery was lying on a quilt beside a fireplace on the floor of a cabin. He saw the flickering of starlight outside a window and felt the warmth of a fire beside him. He noticed his cloak hanging beside the front door and his shoes sitting beneath it. Avery sat up against the wall.

"Are ye feelin' all right now?" the black haired man asked.

Avery nodded drowsily.

"What's yer name then lad?" inquired the other.

"Avery Smith, to my dismay."

The younger man groaned.

"Englishman," the other man growled.

"Yer people are no' particularly…liked by all in Ireland, Englishman," the younger explained.

"I am exceedingly sorry," Avery groaned himself and lay back. He rubbed his forehead and the memory of the three men and the merchant returned to him. "Forgive me, but I must leave." He tried to stand but they pressed him back.

"Ye've a knot on yer 'ead the size of a duck's egg. At least eat some'at first."

Avery shook his head emphatically, making it ache all the more.

The older man leaned back; his scrutinizing eyes burned into Avery's. "And what makes yee so anxious ta leave, lad?"

Avery sighed. What did he have to lose? "I'm wanted back in England and I'm fairly sure I have three drunkard fishermen and a merchant chasing me."

The two glanced at one another and the younger raised an eyebrow. "Are ye a murderer?" he asked.

"No!"

"A kidnapper?" guessed the other.

"No!" Avery felt his cheeks burn with irritation. "I *was* a thief, but I'm through with that life. It has brought me nothing." He looked at the floor awkwardly.

The younger man pulled the older to his feet. They went to a corner in the back of the room and began discussing in heated whispers. They returned in a few moments, the older looking slightly agitated.

"A'm Tom Haddley," the younger one began, "and this is my brother, Gilbert."

"Gilly," the older sibling added.

Tom began again. "If ye wants, then we'll be helpin' ye by letting ye stay here, Englishman."

Avery glanced at them both in disbelief before nodding his head. He could not comprehend why these two men were being so generous to him. He had done nothing for them and had offered nothing in return for their kindnesses.

"Ye'll be workin' for me," Gilly informed him, "as a farm'and while Tom is at the print shop." His arms were crossed and he was half glaring half grinning at Avery. Then he held out his hand. Avery grasped it firmly.

Avery awoke at dawn once again the next morning. He had slept on a pallet by the fireplace while the brothers slept in a separate room containing two beds and a single chest of clothing.

Tom was at the table mixing biscuit batter. "Good morrow te ye, Englishman."

"Hullo. Is that coffee?" Avery asked as he caught the vaguely familiar sent on the air. He had only had coffee twice before and was anxious to try it again.

Tom nodded over his shoulder. "'elp yoursel'." Avery took a mug from the shelf and poured himself a portion from the steaming kettle. "Ye'll have to excuse my brother."

"Hm?"

"Gilly." Tom began rolling the dough out on the table. "'e's a wee bit touchy now and then, especially 'round English."

"Then why are you letting me stay here? I get the feeling I'll only bring trouble."

"As long as yer fisherman donna' show A don't think there will be any problems, Englishman," Tom smiled.

"Where is Gilly?" Avery asked, sipping his coffee.

"Still abed, but 'e'll be up soon." His stirring of the dough slowed and he hesitated before venturing a question. "Who's ring is it, Englishman?"

Avery looked up sharply. So they had found the ring in his shoe. "Personal."

Tom raised his eyebrows significantly.

"I didn't steal it, I assure you. It's just…personal."

Tom seemed to accept this answer and let the subject be.

Gilly was up in an hour and they all sat down to a breakfast of biscuits and honey. Avery reached for a biscuit but Tom kicked him lightly under the table. Avery looked up and saw the brothers bowing their heads. Avery was puzzled but followed suit and soon heard Gilly saying, "Lord, we ask that you grant us wisdom and strength as we go through this day-"

What is he doing? Avery wondered irritably, *I thought we were going to eat.* About that time Gilly stopped speaking and they all raised their heads. Avery reached for a biscuit once again and they all ate ravenously.

Tom left for his job at the *Chronicler*, the newsletter in the town up the road just after breakfast. The other two went out and Gilly handed Avery a shovel.

"Clean out t'e stalls," he ordered, "then put in fresh hay. Watch out fer Day though; she kicks." He gestured to a white horse with a blond mane and tail beside Pinpoint.

Avery looked at Gilly quizzically. "Day?"

He nodded. "Night is Tom's horse and Day is mine. She's Night's Mater. " Gilly turned on his heel and strode away.

Avery stared at his shovel in disgust. Pinpoint neighed to him questioningly. "What are you looking at?" Avery spat.

Suddenly a thought came into his mind. Avery looked about to be sure that Gilly was out of sight and then climbed the ladder to the hay loft. There, he tossed the shovel aside and sat in a pile of hay, which emitted a small cloud of dust. He removed his left shoe and produced his mother's ring. Avery knew that he needed a place to hide this beloved keepsake. He began looking about as if expecting a secret drawer to appear before him; and it did, in a manner of speaking. Avery spied a board in the corner with one end protruding above the floor. He made his way to it and knelt on the dusty floor. The short plank lifted easily, revealing a compartment about a foot long. He placed the handkerchief-encased ring into the small space. After a moment's decision, he placed Ms. Manny's Bible beside it.

After covering the secret with the plank and a mound of hay, Avery took up his shovel and went at his task with a gusto.

The next three days were about the same. Gilly gave Avery as many repulsive jobs as he could; cleaning out the stalls, pig sty, and chicken house full of hens that seemed bent on pecking him to death. Tom left for Echo Falls, a bit of a town some miles north of Dublin, after breakfast each morning and arrived back at five-thirty every afternoon.

After dinner, Tom and Gilly would sit at the table and read from their Bible. They invited Avery to sit with them and do the same. Avery always declined to do so. He thought back to when he had attempted to read Ms. Manny's Bible. His pride refused to let the Haddley's think he was unintelligent in any way.

"Ye'll wish ye had, Englishman," Tom would always insist. Avery just slipped into bed with aching muscles and a sore back.

The next day was Saturday and they awoke to find a thick blanket of snow on the ground. Avery borrowed some gloves and socks from Tom and the two of them bailed fresh hay for the horses and spread seed for the chickens. Gilly hitched Day and Tom's black horse, Night, to a wooden cart.

"Here." Gilly handed Avery a copper shilling.

Avery stared at it dumbly. "What's this?"

"Ye're monthly pay. Coom on."

Gilly and Tom jumped into the cart seat while Avery sat in back with a crate of eggs and a load of firewood. Gilly steered the horses onto the road. Within sight of the Haddley cottage, they came to a fork in the path and turned left.

Ahead of them stretched a wide street with homes and stores on either side. At the bend in the road past the town was a church. A group of children ran along the road chasing a puppy. Some older men sat in chairs on the porch of an old inn and tavern called the Irish Tankard smoking pipes and talking of old times. Women bartered for fabrics and groceries while men haggled for tools. In the wide common in the center of the street, people stood with their carts and wheelbarrows shouting the prices of their goods.

Gilly directed Day and Night into a vacant corner of the common. "Ye and Avery take these te Mr. O'Malley," he ordered and handed the crate of eggs to Tom. "A'll get this firewood sold and then we'll head home. And Avery?"

Smith looked around at him.

"Ye may want to muffle that accent of yers," Gilly warned.

"He thinks *I* have an accent," he mumbled with a roll of his grey eyes.

"We sell the eggs to Mr. O'Malley fur his store every week," Tom explained as they tramped through the snow back down the street.

Avery looked about at the vast number of people. "I'm surprised that the snow didn't keep them indoors." Shivering, he pulled his own cloak tighter around his shoulders.

"Ah," Tom grinned, "this es nothing. It'll melt by tomorrow."

They stopped in front of a store with a sign that read O'Malley's Goods above the door. A small bell jingled as Avery pushed the door open.

A tall man with a long, scraggly beard and flaming red hair stood behind a counter along the west wall. "Good mornin' to ye, lads," he boomed in a bellowing bass voice.

"Good day, Mr. O'Malley," Tom smiled and placed the crate, stuffed with hay and eggs, on the counter. "Thes is Avery Smith. He'll be stayin' with Tom and me for a while."

"Gud to meet ye, sair."

Mr. O'Malley gave Avery a strange look but said nothing to him. "A see ye've brought me some eggs, Mr. Haddley."

Avery began wandering around the store while the two men talked. The store was lined with shelves and barrels of various items; parchments, fabrics, nails, etc. He soon came upon some shirts for sale. Looking ruefully at his own tattered clothing, he decided to spend a portion of his salary on a new one. Avery reached out to retrieve the item for closer inspection. His hand collided unexpectedly with someone else's.

"Oh!"

Avery looked up and saw a young lady, whom he hadn't noticed before, standing beside him.

"Beggin' yer pardon, sair," she said sheepishly. Her hair looked as if it were spun of gold and her eyes were hazel with gold flecks in them. She looked about eighteen and had a very pretty face with skin hewn of ivory. Her clothing carried the faintest scent of lavender about her person.

"Pardon me," Avery mumbled, stumbling over his new-found accent. He now noticed that she had a cloth in her hand and was dusting the shelves. He stepped back to let her pass with a swish of her stiff skirts.

"Ye're new here, are ye not?"

Avery chuckled a little. "A suppose et's obvious."

"Oh, aye," she grinned cheekily.

Avery smiled and continued browsing about the shelves; however, he could not help but watch the girl from the corner of his eye. There was a thought in the back of Avery's mind that he had met her before.

Tom stepped to Avery's side. "A've finished here. What about you?"

"A'll look around a bit more," Avery answered with a shrug.

Tom nodded. "Meet ye back at t'e cart then, eh." He clapped Avery on the back and exited the store with a jingle. The door slammed shut and gave way to an eerie silence. The man behind the counter ventured into a back room. Avery fiddled with a box of nails as he watched the young lady. Where had he seen her?

The girl turned sharply. "Is there something A can help ye with, Mr.-"

"Avery Smith."

"Well, pardon me Mr. Smith," she half whispered, "but ye've been starin' at…those nails for a while now." She finished with a shrug.

Avery nodded and placed the box back on the shelf. "A'm sorry A stared, Miss. It's just-"

"Amelia."

"Excuse meh?"

The girl's eyes seemed to be smiling at him although her face held a puzzled expression. "Me name is Amelia Bairns. And ye've no need for the accent 'round me, Englishman, for ye've not yet mastered et."

"Ms. Bairns," Avery began but couldn't finish. Not only was he surprised that she had seen through his accent, but he had just realized where he remembered her from. They watched each other awkwardly for a moment.

"Mia!" The shout from the back room made them both jump.

"Yes, Uncle Nate?" Amelia sighed and turned toward the door.

The man poked his bushy red head out into the store. "Time for ye te head on home now, girl."

"Yes, Uncle Nate." Amelia began untying her apron strings.

"May I walk you home, Ms. Bairns?"

Amelia smiled as she pulled a cloak over her shoulders. "Ye may, Mr. Smith."

Amelia's house was just beyond the church, tucked away in a small grove of trees. Avery was looking ahead but Amelia watched him as they walked. "So what part of England are ye from, Mr. Smith?"

He hesitated, not sure if he should tell her that he was from Lancashire. "Over the hills and far away," Avery replied roguishly.

"A can't put me finger on it," Amelia half whispered, "but A feel as if A know ye from somewhere. Yer face seems familiar, somehow."

They passed through the gate at the end of the dirt path to Amelia's front door. When they reached the door, Amelia turned to face him. "*Have* A met ye before?" she inquired uncertainly.

Avery tried to keep a smile from his lips. "Good day, fair maiden." He turned on his heel.

Amelia turned to enter her house but stopped short. She looked over her shoulder. "The man from the market."

"Yes," he regarded her with a curious look. Amelia's face had turned pallid.

"But, ye were-" Her voice trembled. "-blind."

"No," Avery shook his head nonchalantly. "I was never blind."

"Then whi-"

"I, ah," Avery stuttered. He tried to look into her eyes, but he could not. "I cannot lie to you again. I had just gotten out of jail and I didn't want people to recognize me."

"So ye lied." There was a tinge of anger in Amelia's words. "And what were ye in jail for?" Now she raised her voice a little.

Avery swallowed. *I shouldn't have told her*, he thought. "I-I was a thief."

"A lier and a thief. Do Tom and Gilly know of thes?"

"Yes, but-"

She turned and opened the door.

"Ms. Bairns, wait-"

"Good day, sair!" she spat and slammed the door.

Avery ran his fingers through his hair. He trudged away toward town as tiny flakes of snow began to fall.

Avery awoke Sunday morning and had a breakfast of pancakes with Tom and Gilly.

"Ye'll need to borrow a shirt from me," Tom said without looking up from his meal.

"Hm?" Avery looked at the brothers in surprise.

"Fer church," Tom answered.

Avery glanced at Gilly and poked at his cakes. "I think I'll skip it, thanks."

Gilly's head snapped up. "Ye will not!"

Avery was only mildly surprised at his authoritative tone.

"We canno' make ye read the Bible or join our faith, but you're coming to church wit' us, lad."

Avery sighed but did not argue. Forty-five minutes later, he was sitting atop Pinpoint with Tom and Gilly beside him astride their own mounts. As they approached the church, they saw a crowd of people entering before them. Avery tied his horse to the fence post alongside his companions'.

"Good day t' ye, Mia."

Avery heard Tom speak and immediately turned to see Amelia Bairns approaching them. "Good mornin' Tom, Gilly," she smiled sweetly.

Avery stepped up beside her nervously. "Hello, Miss Bairns."

Amelia turned a hard eye to him. She spoke quietly to Gilly and Tom. "Excuse us, please." A command, not a request. Gilly looked sharply at Avery and Tom raised an eyebrow questioningly before they moved slowly away.

"Mr. Smith," Amelia began when they had gone, "I-"

"Wait, please Ms. Bairns." Avery surprised even himself with this interruption. "You were right in what you said yesterday. My reputation as a thief has followed me thus far, but I assure you that I want to change that."

Amelia's face was hard and her lips were pursed, but her eyes seemed soft and compassionate. Avery continued his earnest speech. "That is not my life anymore. I want to earn my food, not steal it. You don't have to believe me, but I hope you will…despite the fact that I'm English." Amelia's breath seemed to catch in her throat. "I would like to get to know you." This last statement slipped unchecked from Avery's lips and, without waiting for a reply, he walked toward the door of the church.

"Mia."

Avery turned, startled by Amelia's voice. "Call me Mia," she spoke without turning, "everyone else does."

Avery nodded, smiled, and entered the church. He tried to pay attention to the fervently delivered sermon, but his mind was constantly wandering to the flaxen haired lady in front of him. After the service had ended, they hurried home.

Avery tossed and turned restlessly in his bed that night. He could not sleep for his mind raced with thoughts of Mia. After many attempts, he finally drifted into a light slumber. His dreams, however, were just as restless as his body.

In his mind, Avery saw himself as a child. His uncle, whom he had not thought about in years, came and stood beside him. Without warning, Avery plunged into a hole that appeared beneath him. The shadowy face of his uncle peered down at him. "Why didn't you catch me?" Avery yelled up at him. His uncle walked away without a word. Next it was Amelia's face that looked down at him. She seemed distraught and Avery could see the liquid sorrow in her eyes. "Come to me!" she cried. Avery began grasping at the walls of the hole in an attempt to climb upward, but the loose dirt broke away in his hands. He soon gave up. He lifted his arms toward her. "Give me your hand, Mia!" She shook her head fervently. "A will fall in." Then she was gone. Avery slumped in sadness, but then the hand of his uncle reached down to him and filled his vision.

Avery startled awake. He sighed wearily and rolled onto his back while he rubbed his eyes with spindly fingers. His forehead was moist with anxious perspiration. Slowly, the light notes of some musical instrument reached him. Avery sat up and looked around. The tones of a flute or pipe seemed to be coming from outside. Avery crept to the peg by the back door and pulled his cloak about his shoulders. Then, after slipping into his soft leather shoes, he peaked through the crack in Tom and Gilly's bedroom door.

Gilly lay sleeping soundly but Tom's bed was vacant.

Avery stepped through the back door. A misty rain was falling over the Irish countryside but in the moonlight it appeared to be a thick fog. Already the rain was freezing into tiny ice crystals. Through the haze, Avery espied Tom's silhouette sitting with his back against a tree.

Tom ceased playing his flute and looked up as Avery approached. "Did A wake ye, Englishman?" he wondered aloud.

"Hardly." Avery sat beside his friend and rubbed at his long arms for warmth. "I didn't know you played an instrument."

"Ah," Tom grinned, "et's just an old pipe o' my father's. Not even sure what it is." He lifted it to his lips and trilled out a few notes.

Neither of them spoke for some time. They sat watching rain water drip from the leaves of the tree. "It was a good church service thes mornin'," Tom remarked. Avery shrugged. "Why do ye turn from it?"

Avery kept his eyes to the ground and pondered silently. "There was never anyone to teach religion to me after…after my mother died," he sighed lamely. "And I guess I just never had a need for it."

Tom shook his head and did not speak for a little while. "But there are those who will teach et to ye now, Avery. Why don't ye listen?"

It was strange to hear his name on the lips of this Irishman and even stranger that he could think so calmly in the middle of this particular discussion. Avery did not have an answer.

"There is life after death, Avery. Perhaps ye should start thinkin' about yers."

Avery jumped to his feet and began walking swiftly toward the house. Behind him he heard Tom's flute being played into the cold night.

Chapter 6
Christmas

Avery sat astride Pinpoint as he trotted along the dusty road to Echo Falls. Gilly had given him permission to go to town in search of a more adequate shirt. *"This es a mild winter,"* he had commented, *"but A suppose that shirt of yours es a bit thin."*

So now he was stepping over the threshold of O'Malley's Goods. Avery quickly selected a thick, white shirt and placed it on the counter. "Is Ms. Mia not working today, siar?" Avery queried, careful to accent his voice.

Mia's red-haired uncle looked up. "Ye just missed her."

Avery nodded and gathered up the shirt as he placed his shilling on the counter. Mr. O'Malley handed him his change—two pence—and waved him out the door. Just as young Smith was tucking the garment into a borrowed saddlebag, he spotted Mia across the street. A man with thick black hair all matted under his hat was pursuing her.

"A'll not leave till ye give me an answer, Mia," he was saying in a gruff voice.

"A've given ye the answer more than once, Jake O'Shea!" Mia exclaimed. "Go find you'self a wee tap maid!"

"Wrong answer, luv." O'Shea's face darkened and he grabbed Mia's elbow.

"Sair," Avery stepped between the two and removed O'Shea's hold on Mia. "A don't believe the lady wants t' talk to ye."

"Tha's not for ye to say," he sneered.

"Do ye want t' talk to him, Ms. Mia?" Avery asked over his shoulder.

"No!" was all Mia said and O'Shea slumped away with a darkened countenance.

Avery turned to face Mia. "Who was that, Ms. Mia?"

"A suitor, if ye could call 'im that. He's been after my hand for a year now at least."

"Perhaps he'll stay away for a while."

"Thank ye, Mr. Smith," she whispered, the tension showing in her fair face.

"Don't thank me yet. He might come back."

Mia's face broke into a pretty smile. "Ah, but blessed are t'e peacemakers, Mr. Smith."

Avery laughed. "So it would seem but there are times when I would doubt it."

Mia's face changed again to an expression of astonishment. "Ye would doubt the Bible, sair?" she breathed. Avery was taken aback by this accusation. "Matthew chapter five, verse nine," she recited. *"Blessed are the peacemakers for they shall be called the children of God."*

"Oh," Avery huffed, feeling slightly perturbed with his embarrassment. They began walking toward Mia's home in an uncomfortable silence. When they were half-way there, Avery mustered up the courage to speak. "If you don't mind me asking, Ms. Mia, why were you in England when I first met you?"

"A was visiting an aunt who had taken ill," she explained quietly and then added, "She died soon after I left."

"A am sorry, Mr. Smith."

Mia went on lightly. "It's just me and ma parents, now. Well, except for my Uncle Nate and his family."

Avery nodded somberly.

"And you?" the lady wondered. "Where is your family?"

Avery looked at the ground. "My father died in a duel when I was young. My mother died when I was twelve." He saw Mia glance at him from the corner of his eye. "I have an uncle back in Lancashire," he remarked. The last thing he wanted was for her to feel sorry for him.

"Would ye like to have dinner with me and my family, Mr. Smith?" Mia inquired.

"Does this mean that you wish to be...friends with me?"

A smile tickled her lips. "It does."

Avery grinned. "I would, Ms. Mia."

As they approached, Avery noticed a man working in the garden beside the house. "Father!" Mia called to him. The man looked up and Avery saw that his face was a sea of wrinkles wreathed in snowy hair. Mia ran ahead and embraced him.

"Mia," he laughed, "A see ye've brought company."

"Father, this is Avery Smith," she said and gestured in his direction.

Mia's father held out his hand. "Ian Bairns."

Avery took his hand and almost winced in the older man's firm grasp. "Pleasure, sair."

"A have invited Mr. Smith to stay for dinner, Father," Mia smiled.

He nodded amiably. "Go and show Mr. Smith to the barn then, girl, while A warn ye're mater to set the table for four."

Avery followed Mia to a small one-story stable with Pinpoint trailing behind them. The barn had four stalls and Avery noticed a grey mare watching them from one of these.

"That's my horse," Mia told him. "Her name is Mari." The flick of a tail and the appearance of another horse's muzzle warned Avery that two of the other stalls were occupied as well. "That's Pete and Pat," Mia explained. "My parent's horses."

Avery smiled but a disturbing thought had just occurred to him. "Ms. Mia," he began as he latched the door to Pinpoint's stall, "have you told your parents of my reputation?"

The smile fell from her face and she turned her hazel eyes down toward the floor. "No."

Avery was puzzled when he heard this. "Why?"

"A believed ye that day when ye said ye wanted to change," she whispered and looked back up at him. "Was A wrong to do so?" she demanded sharply.

"No."

Mia smiled at his boyish indignance. "And what is et that has made ye wish to change, Mr. Smith?"

Avery dove into the tale that he had kept to himself for so long. "When I was a lad, just after me mother died, I ran away from my uncle's home. I was determined to make a life for myself better than my mother had been able to give me. We had lost everything and had been living on the street for four years."

Mia's eyes glistened. "A'm sorry."

Avery waved the words away unconcernedly. "To make a long story short, instead of making my life better I made it worse by becoming a thief."

"And now what do ye plan to do with et?"

Avery shrugged. Before he could say anything more, they heard Mia's mother calling to them.

Mia smiled. "Shall we go inside now, or do you plan to eat with the horses?"

Avery laughed dryly. "Don't snub it until you've tried it." He could have bitten his tongue off. Mia watched him oddly, as though trying to decide if this was meant as a joke. Avery turned slightly and scratched his eyebrow in an effort to hide the heat in his cheeks.

Amelia led the way to the back door. "Mother?"

Mrs. Bairns bustled forward and kissed her daughter's cheek. "How do ye do?" she greeted Avery before Mia could speak. "A'm Lenore Bairns." The lady's hair was red, though not as fiery as her brother's. She was heavy set and kindly. Avery perceived immediately the source of Mia's indescribable eyes.

"Mah pleasure, ma'am," he greeted and kissed the lady's hand.

Amelia, he learned had grown up in Echo Falls and often looked after her uncle's children, Benny and Ann O'Malley. Only one thing occurred during dinner that was of any consequence. Avery sat across from Mia and reached for the potatoes.

Mrs. Bairns had whacked his hand with a wooden spoon and said, "Grace first, Mr. Smith." Avery, feeling immensely foolish, bowed his head and did not reach for another thing until Mia did.

"I hope ye enjoyed yourself, Mr. Smith," Mia said as Avery led Pinpoint from his stall.

"A did Ms. Mia. Thank ye for havin' me."

Amelia wrinkled her nose. "Must ye really use that accent around me, Mr. Smith?"

"You think I am too cautious?"

"Aye. At least around me."

"And your parents? Should I be worried about them?"

She answered his questions with a question of her own. "Perhaps ye would like to come again next week after Christmas?"

"I would." Avery found that his hand was fidgeting with Pinpoint's bridle. "Maybe we could take a walk afterward."

She nodded happily and Avery felt as though he could stand and watch her all day. However, he was forced to turn swiftly and clear his throat when it was attacked by a sudden itch.

"Do ye have a cold?"

"No, just a dry throat," Avery hastily insisted.

"An' where's yer handkerchief?"

"I don't have one." Mia's face turned comically severe and she placed her hands on her hips. Avery laughed roguishly and swung onto the saddle. "Good day, Ms. Mia."

"Good day to ye, Avery Smith."

Avery cantered away on Pinpoint and vaguely wondered if Gilly would be put out with him for being away so long.

Amelia cracked open the front door on Christmas Day. A small knock had drawn her there with a shawl wrapped over her dress. She perceived the back of a retreating figure through the thick gusts of snow, but he was soon lost to sight in the flurries. Mia opened the door wider and something on the porch caught her eye.

Three rosebuds lay amidst some scattered snowflakes bound together with a ribbon. Mia lifted them gingerly along with the bit of parchment beneath them. On bud was white, another red, and the last yellow, all tied with a pale pink ribbon. Her curiosity sparked, she looked to the parchment and read the painstakingly written script;

Ms. Mia,

The white is to show your serene gentleness
The red is your undeniable beauty
The yellow is the light in your eyes

Happy Christmas,
Avery Smith

Mia's breath caught in her throat. She shivered and closed the door, half wishing that Avery had stayed.

"Thank ye, Tom," Gilly said as he held up the new bridal his brother had given him. "A needed a new one." Tom smiled with pleasure as he pulled on the new coat that Gilly had bought for him.

Avery grinned broadly and tossed him a small package covered in discarded issues of the *Chronicler*. "That's for you and Gilly."

"From who, A wonder," Tom teased as he ripped at the paper. The wrappings fell away to reveal a small wooden chest with the name HADDLEY etched on its lid.

Gilly ran his fingers over the name. "Did ye carve thes yerself?"

Avery nodded. "But I swiped your penknife to do it." He let his voice slide into a chuckle.

Gilly raised an eyebrow as he handed Avery a thin, cylindrical package. Avery tore at the paper and discovered a flute similar to Tom's.

"Try et out," the latter urged.

Avery held the instrument to his lips and blew out a few sharp notes. He winced and lowered the pipe quickly.

"Ye'll get et," Tom assured as he produced a small paper sack. "Thes came for ye yesterday." He handed it to Avery, who reached in and removed a sheet of stationary. He noticed the letters *AB* stamped on the seal as he broke it and read the message;

Dear Mr. Smith,

My family and I invite you to dinner at seven this Friday, weather permitting. I hope you will join us.

Happy Christmas,
Mia

Avery could not help but grin and the brothers noticed a wistful gleam in his eye. They exchanged glances but said nothing. "It's from Mia," Avery told them needlessly.

"Really," Gilly mused dryly. Avery ignored him and removed a neatly folded handkerchief from the bag. When he spread the white linen flat, he discovered a silver penny within its folds.

The blizzard lasted for two weeks, making it impossible for Avery to attend dinner with the Bairnses. Luckily, by the third week the snow stopped, leaving a thick blanket on the ground in its wake. Avery spent most of the next three days with Tom and Gilly clearing paths to the barn and chicken house and the road. They bailed extra hay for the horses and built a new roof over the chicken house to ensure that melting snow would not make its way through any small crevices. After those three days of hard work, he saddled Pinpoint and set out over the snow drifts toward the Bairns residence. Echo falls glistened in the afternoon sunlight. The town seemed deserted except for a group of children. They ran by hurling snowballs at one another. Pinpoint started a bit with a twirl of his tail.

"All right, calm down," Avery soothed and stroked the horse's mane. "I know your restless."

"Ha!"

Smith turned sharply. He did not like the sound of that.

Jake O'Shea stood in front of one of the buildings. His face was strangely gleeful and his hands were clasped behind his back. He cut an interesting figure with his chin jutting upward in an open show of arrogance.

Avery looked him up and down distastefully. "May A help ye wit' something, sair?"

"Oh, drop et!" O'Shea spat. "A knew A smelled something amiss when yew came along!"

"And just what was that, sair?" Avery was rapidly becoming very impatient.

"Stop the accent ye filthy Englishman!"

Chapter 7
Mia Bairns and Echo Falls

Jake O'Shea performed his vengeful task promptly and effectively. Within two days the entire town of Echo Falls was in an uproar about the English liar. Tom said it was simply O'Shea's way of avenging his gruff encounter with Avery.

"O'Shea is just angry 'e canna have Ms. Mia, so 'e attacked ye instead. Et'll all blow over in a week er two," he would say every time one of the townspeople would look Avery up and down disgustedly.

Somehow Tom's words were not much of a comfort. Although Avery had to admit that it was a relief to be able to abdicate his rather pathetic and tedious accent. And there was also the fact that Mia and her parents understood.

"These are difficult times, Mr. Smith," Mia's father had said. "Et was na' right, what ye did, but it is forgiven ye. In time t'e others will see that too."

Avery now sat on Mia's front porch conversing with her father while Mia cleaned up the dinner dishes with her mother.

"A've seen ye at church, Mr. Smith," Ian Bairns said suddenly. "A assume that ye've been saved." The statement was meant as a question. The man was probing him.

"Well," Avery began, treading lightly, "to an extent, sir."

Mr. Bairns leaned back and studied young Smith. The latter could not help but notice that there was a stern gleam in Ian's eyes. "A must tell you Mr. Smith, that ye're answer is most distressing," he said quietly, "especially since ye have been calling on mah daughter."

Avery stared dumbly. "I…"

At that moment, Mia stepped out onto the porch.

"Ms. Mia." Avery stood swiftly, very glad for the interruption.

Mia smiled but watched him with strange curiosity, as though she sensed his discomfiture. "Mr. Smith."

"I'm afraid I must be going," Avery declared with slumped shoulders. "The dinner was wonderful, thank you."

"A'll walk ye to the barn," Mia insisted.

Avery nodded to her. "Good evening, Mr. Bairns."

Ian said nothing but stood slowly with an almost sorrowful countenance.

Avery pulled up the hood of his cloak and waited for Mia to retrieve hers before stepping into the light mist that was falling in the pale light of dusk. They were half way to the barn before Mia spoke.

"Is something t'e matter, Mr. Smith?"

"No," he lied quietly, "not at all." He felt a pang of guilt at lying to this lady, something that did not happen very often. Avery untethered Pinpoint and led him out to where Mia was waiting. "Good evening-" Avery began but stopped short.

Amelia was staring up at him. Her eyes seemed to dance in the moonlight and Avery's heart flipped in his chest. A trickle of rain slid down her cheek from the hair that was plastered to her forehead with moisture. In that moment Avery understood what his heart had been telling him for the past few weeks. His limbs began to tremble with nervousness. It was then that he saw that she too had happiness in her eyes.

"Good evening, Mr. Smith," Mia uttered, but neither of them moved.

Avery heard Pinpoint stomp irritably. He ignored the animal. He leaned toward Mia. Their eyes were locked and neither of them could turn away...neither of them wanted to. Then, suddenly—inexplicably—Avery stopped. Mia's look turned to one of anxiousness; almost fear. He saw her breath turn into steam in the chilly night air and felt it blow against his chin. But there was something wrong. He had wanted to kiss her, had to kiss her, but something was making him stop. Something was telling him that if he did this thing, he would regret it forever.

Avery turned away and swung himself onto Pinpoint's back. He rode away as fast as he could go and never looked back.

Avery lept into the wagon beside Tom. Across the street, Mia Bairns was stepping out of O'Malley's. Avery watched as she noticed him, turned, and walked quickly in the opposite direction.

The wagon lurched into motion as he sighed, "She's avoiding me."

"What's that?" Tom looked at him strangely.

Avery shrugged the question away with a lie. Always a lie. "Nothing." He turned to Gilly, who was sitting in the seat. "Do you mind if I take the afternoon off?"

"S'pose not." Gilly directed the horses to the barn. "Just be back by dark."

Avery nodded, and, as soon as they pulled into the barn, he made his way up to the loft. There was something he had to retrieve before he left to find Mia. If he was to begin a different life, he must start somewhere.

Avery had just caught sight of her house when he saw Mia sitting sidesaddle atop her grey horse. He halted Pinpoint and watched her ride into the forest at a trot. "Come on," he whispered to Pinpoint and followed Mia's lead.

She was not hard to track. The foot-path was speckled with recent hoof marks leading through the forest. Avery trotted along the curves of the trail, feeling the twisting of his own nervous stomach all the way. The bare trees made the forest seem strangely eerie and foreboding. Soon the sounds of rushing water filled his ears. Finally the trees opened up into a clearing below a short cliff. The cliff itself was a tower of boulders rising ten feet above a flowing stream. A majestic waterfall spilled over the edge and cascaded into the babbling waters below. The sun shot through the fall in a prism of rainbows. *Perfect*, Avery thought and smiled to himself as he took in the beauty of the falls.

He spotted Amelia's horse, Mari, grazing by the trees while Mia herself was perched on a large rock by the river's edge. Her shoes lay beside her seat and her feet were tucked under her dress. She looked so out of place in the cold forest. Avery stared at the back of her head for a moment, swallowed, and dismounted. Mia only turned her head slightly at the sound.

He walked slowly to her side. "May I join you?"

Mia nodded her permission and Avery lowered himself onto the rock beside her. "A was just reading."

This statement drew Avery's attention to the Bible that lay open in Mia's lap.

They sat quietly for a time watching the water and Mia looked back toward her Bible. He leaned toward Mia and read over her shoulder. He skimmed a few lines and slumped back.

She turned to him curiously. "Is something wrong?"

Avery tried to hide his frustration and waved the question away carelessly. "No, not at all." Always a lie.

Mia was silently playing with the ribbon she used as a bookmark in her Bible. "Is that why ye donna read the Book, Avery?" She spoke quietly, but Avery was so startled that she might as well have shouted. Her face softened now as she waited for his answer. "Because ye donna understand?"

The question was very irksome to him; however, Avery could not help but like it when she used his first name. He just smiled and looked to the noble fall. "What is this place?" he asked, clearly avoiding the question.

Mia seemed disappointed but replied, "This es Echo Falls. A often come here to read." The magnificent splendor of the fall entranced Avery. When he looked back at Mia she was staring blankly at the rushing stream water.

Avery reached into his pocket and pulled out the wooden flute he had received for Christmas. He lifted it to his lips and began to play softly. The notes seemed to hang in the air and beat in rhythm with the water fall. Mia closed her eyes and listened wistfully to the flowing crescendo of Avery's music.

"That was beautiful," she commented when he lowered the pipe.

He shrugged and grinned modestly. "Not half as beautiful as you."

Mia's back went rigid and she turned sharply as if to speak. Avery beat her to it. "Amelia, you are the most wonderful woman I have ever met. You're pretty, smart-"

"Avery please-" A look of terror was etched on the lady's pale countenance.

"I feel as if I must speak or I shall burst." He paused and forced down the lump of nervousness in his throat. "Do you remember that night by the barn the last time I visited? That was the night that I saw what it is I am feeling and that you feel it too." Mia's eyes narrowed as she tried to hold back tears. She looked away from Avery toward the falling water. "I love you Mia; I always will. I'll care for you until the day I die-" he reached into his pocket and brought his mother's ring out into the light, "if you'll have me and take my ring."

Mia stared at the ring breathlessly before turning her tear-streaked face toward Avery.

"I beg you to say it."

"What?" Mia was just as breathless as he felt.

"I know that you love me, Mia."

She swallowed. "A fear you are mistaken, sair."

"How can you say that?" Avery demanded in complete bewilderment.

"If ye had asked me a week ago," she croaked in a husky voice, "A would have said yes…and we would have regretted it for the rest of our lives."

All the happiness in Avery's heart drained away like the swiftly moving water.

"Avery," Mia tried to explain, "A can not marry a man who does not share my faith."

"I would go to church every Sunday," he insisted hastily.

Amelia shook her head weakly. "Yer body would, but yer heart wouldna'."

Avery stared at her incredulously. "What have I done to change your mind in the past week?"

"It is what ye have not done. I thought that ye shared my faith, but my father has told me differently." Avery clutched the ring with trembling hands. Mia placed a hand on his arm. "A'm so sorry, Avery. A have brought this upon us both. A was wrong to assume…If A had asked all the questions A should have asked from the beginning then it never would have gone this far."

"But you love me…I know you love me."

Mia's eyes looked pained and she averted them carefully. "A fear you are mistaken, sair. For I cannot."

Avery turned away from her as the hot tears rushed to his eyes. He felt the heat rise in his cheeks and then drain away into cold nothingness. His breath stuck in his chest, and, when he regained it, it came with a bitter chuckle. "Remove your hand good lady," he ordered with eyes that blazed into hers. "I wouldn't want it to be soiled by the rags of a thief." He slid off the cold rock and started toward Pinpoint.

"Avery, wait!" Mia called after him. "If ye would but listen-"

It was too late. Her shouts receded into the distance as Avery galloped away. In his gray, searching eyes, Amelia was lost to him forever more. And there was nothing he could do to bring her back.

Tom discovered Avery in the barn hayloft at sundown. When he had not shown up for supper, Tom had gone looking for his friend. Avery had his back to the wall and was turning a small object in his hands.

"Hullo, Tom," Avery greeted him dryly, keeping his eyes on the thing in his hands. Tom climbed the ladder and sat in front of Avery. After a minute, the latter spoke. "You once asked me why I turn from Christianity." Now Avery looked Tom in the eye. "But why do you keep it?"

Tom was thoughtful and for a moment he did not speak. He seemed to be choosing his words very carefully. "For salvation. And because I know where I want to spend my eternity." He paused and studied Avery's blunt stare.

"But he answered and said, It is written, man shall not live by bread alone, but by every word that proceedeth out of the mouth of God. Matthew 4:4." Avery continued to stare at him blankly. "It's from the Bible, Avery. Ephesians 4:28; *Let him that stole steal no more: but rather let him labor, working with his hands the thing which is good, that he may have to give to him that needeth.*"

"But I'm not a thief anymore, Tom," Avery muttered irritably, turning his face away.

"Did ye ever think that might not be enough? The only reason ye were forced to hide here in Ireland is because ye were on the run. And ye saw a life that ye wanted. The point I am trying to make," Tom said with flashing eyes, "is that ye have sins Avery, and unless ye repent of those sins then ye'll be condemned. Matthew-"

"Will you *stop* quoting scriptures for once!" Avery shouted in anger.

Tom's look of frustration melted into one of pity. "When are ye going to realize that ye need Him, Avery? Without God ye are lost. When will ye listen?"

Avery glared back at him. "When you start saying things I want to hear."

Tom's face hardened and he sighed. "If A know ye, Avery, that is something that will never happen." Tom turned and stepped down the first few rungs of the ladder.

"Tom wait!" Avery called to him despairingly. Tom looked up reluctantly. Avery held up the ring he had been holding. "I want you and Gilly to have this." He held it out and Tom took it gingerly in his palm.

"Avery-"

"It was me mother's," the solemn Smith sighed. "I think she would want you to have it after all the kindness you both have shown me."

Tom nodded slowly and continued down the ladder.

Avery leaned back and closed his eyes, but he could not stem the hot tears that fell that night he spent in the barn. He did not sleep at all.

"Good mornin', Mia," Gilly smiled as he and Tom sat in the pew behind the lady the next morning. "Good mornin' Mr. and Mrs. Bairns."

While Gilly chatted with Mia's parents, she turned to Tom. "Where is Mr. Smith?"

Tom shifted uneasily. "He said he wasn't feeling well."

Amelia would have inquired further, but Mr. Regan was standing up to begin the service.

Mia pressed her heels gently into Mari's side as she trotted up beside the Haddley farm that afternoon. She had taken a shortcut through the woods and emerged beside the house. Mia could not explain why she had come; perhaps she wanted to see if she could help Avery overcome his illness. No, she knew it was something more. And suddenly she was terrified. What would she say to him? The man she had refused.

Mia looked around the backyard from her elevated position in the sidesaddle. Avery was not hard to spot. He was by the barn chopping firewood. Mia shook her head and turned her horse away into the woods.

Tom woke early Monday morning to find that Avery's bed by the fire had not been slept in. He put a pot of coffee over the fire and dressed before heading out the back door.

"Avery?" he hollered tentatively as he made his way to the barn. He really did not expect to receive any kind of answer. He merely expected to see his friend asleep in the hay loft. When he entered the barn, the first thing he noticed was that Pinpoint was missing from his stall. He looked around and espied that fresh hay had been bailed for Night and Day. Tom climbed the ladder, but when he reached the loft it was empty.

Tom realized with a jolt what had happened. "Oh no," he murmured in despair.

Chapter 8
Truth

Avery wiped dew from his eyes with the back of his hand as he urged Pinpoint to greater speeds. He had covered the distance from Echo Falls to the sea in one night and now he was racing along the shoreline. White sand flew in great streaks behind the horse's hooves. The briny air stung his nostrils and his ears were filled with the rushing of the tide. He had to get out of Ireland; he had to be rid of the country that held his heart.

Avery slowed Pinpoint to a trot as he neared the docks by a small town. He slid off the saddle and led Pinpoint along the docks where sailors and fishermen were loading and unloading their boats. He wandered about listening to the many conversations intermingled with the squawks of the seagulls.

"These goods is bound fer Ferns-"
"Fetch me that caulk!"
"So then meh sister said-"
"Fish fer sale!"

Then a clear voice rumbled out in a merry bass. "Aye, I'm bound fer England wit' t'e next tide."

Avery fairly sagged with relief and approached the small sail boat. A short elderly man stood on the deck. His face was so bewhiskered that Avery could hardly see his eyes. "Is this your boat, sir?"

The man grinned jovially. "Aye. Thes is the *Lady of the Lake* and I'm Simeon McKracken."

Avery shook his outstretched hand and tried not to cringe at the sight of McKracken's rotten teeth. "Avery Smith. I heard you say you're bound for England, Mr. McKracken."

Simeon nodded. "To Lancaster within t'e hour."

"Would you mind a passenger?"

Simeon rubbed his whiskers thoughtfully. "I reckon the *Lady* could carry you and yer horse, fer a small price that es."

Avery took out one of the two coins he had in his pocket. "Will a shilling do?"

"Aye!" McKracken agreed eagerly. Avery tossed him the coin and led an anxious Pinpoint onto the deck. "Whoa," Simeon coaxed softly as he tried to help Avery calm the agitated animal. "Why don't ye take that bucket and fetch this fellow some water afore we shove off?"

Avery hesitated, suspecting fraud, but then he noticed the stream within clear view of the boat. He decided to chance it. Simeon never made any move to leave without his passenger, however, and Avery felt guilty for misjudging the old man.

Pinpoint drank his fill while Avery helped Simeon ready the boat. He had no knowledge of sailing, but McKracken instructed him patiently and Avery caught on quick. In half an hour they were sailing out for England.

"Are ye bound for home then, my English friend?" the old sailor wondered gruffly.

"Aye," Smith sighed, his watery gray eyes sweeping the waves ahead of them. "To the only home I'll ever have it seems."

Avery sat in the bow of the *Lady of the Lake* staring up at the night sky. In spite of himself, his thoughts turned to Amelia. She had refused him on moral grounds; on Christian grounds. *But she admitted that she loved me; so what about her faith would make her refuse my proposal?*

Avery stood and walked to where his saddle lay beside Pinpoint. Tied to the saddle horn was a small sack. He opened it and removed the tattered Bible from its folds. He leafed through a few pages carefully. "Mr. McKracken?"

"Call me Simeon," he chuckled from his place at the tiller.

"Simeon, do you know anything about religion?"

Simeon shrugged. "A went to church as a child, but tha's about all."

Avery nodded forlornly and returned to his seat in the bow. There he was rocked to sleep by the gentle motion of the waves.

"'ere we are," Simeon grinned as they sailed into the docks.

Smith helped McKracken tie up to the peer and then led Pinpoint off the boat. "Thank you for the passage, Simeon."

Simeon tipped his hat with a lopsided grin. "Lancaster is about a mile that way. Good luck to ye, Englisher!"

Avery waved from his saddle and galloped away. He had just sighted Lancaster when he veered off the road into a thick wood. He had no desire to be in a big city, at least until he knew he was safe in town. He slumped in his saddle and let Pinpoint walk where he wished. He felt detached from the world, as if everyone else was a part of something that he could not understand.

Pinpoint brought him to the edge of the woods, and Avery finally realized where he was. He looked up and saw the house of Todd Genellsteen and his father. The sun was setting below the horizon as Avery approached. He dismounted nervously and rapped on the door.

The door swung inward to reveal Mr. Genellsteen. His face broke into a wide grin. "Welcome!" Avery was doubly surprised when the shorter man threw his arms around him. "Todd, grab another plate!"

Mr. Genellsteen ushered Avery in while Todd set another place at the table. "I hope I'm not intruding," Avery said quietly.

"Never!" Genellsteen scoffed.

Todd beamed up at him. "Good to see you again, Mr. Smith."

Avery grinned and shook the boy's hand. "And you. It is good to be in England again."

"Oh?" Todd's father said curiously.

The boy became excited and bombarded Avery with questions. "Did you run off to Spain? Italy? Not France I hope. Did you have many adventures, Mr. Smith?"

"Calm down lad," Avery chuckled. "I was in Ireland."

He took a seat at the table and, after a blessing was said, began shoveling in the beef and potatoes. It was not until he smelled the food that he began to feel hungry. No, not just hungry, but famished. He had not felt much of anything other than confusion in the past few days and the rumblings of his stomach had eluded him.

Father and son exchanged glances before the former spoke. "So, what brings you, Mr. Smith?"

Avery barely looked up from his meal. "I wondered," he said around a cheekful of boiled potatoes, "if I might stay the night here." He hesitated and then reached for his bag and removed the Bible. "And I wondered if you could help me with something."

"Certainly."

"Father preaches for the Lancaster Church," Todd informed Avery matter-of-factly.

His father chuckled while Avery stared at him dumbly. He could not believe his luck.

"Now clear the table and head up to bed," he heard Genellsteen say.

After Todd climbed the stairs to his room, Avery slid the Bible toward Genellsteen. "Can you help me to understand this?"

Mr. Genellsteen studied Avery for a moment and stroked his chin reflectively. "You are not saved, Mr. Smith?"

Avery wrinkled his brow in confusion.

"I see." Mr. Genellsteen reached for the Bible and flipped through it until he found what he was looking for. "Have you ever heard of Jesus?"

"I've heard the name," Avery acknowledged. "At church in Echo Falls."

"Ah, so you have had some religion taught you, yes?"

Avery shook his head. "I went but I never listened-" Smith stopped mid-sentence and slumped in his chair. "I never listened to any of them," he whispered vaguely. "They tried to tell me and I just pushed them away every time." He was speaking more to himself than to Mr. Genellsteen. He ran his bony fingers through his hair characteristically.

"Then listen now, lad." Genellsteen looked to the Bible in his hands and began reading. "Matthew 1:18-23; *Now the birth of Jesus Christ was on this wise: When as his mother Mary was espoused to Joseph before they came together, she was found with child of the Holy Ghost. Then Joseph her husband being a just* man, *and not willing to make her a public example, was minded to put her away privily. But while he thought on these things, behold, the angel of the Lord appeared unto him in a dream, saying, Joseph, thou son of David, fear not to take unto thee Mary thy wife: for that which is conceived in her is of the Holy Ghost. And she shall bring forth a son, and thou shalt call his name JESUS: for he shall save his people from their sins. Now all this was done, that it might be fulfilled which was spoken of the Lord by the prophet, saying, Behold a virgin shall be with child, and shall bring forth a son, and they shall call his name Immanuel, which being interpreted is, God with us.*"

Here Genellsteen stopped and repeated, "For he shall save his people from their sins. Jesus, the son of God, was sent here to save us, Avery."

"Save us from what?" Avery wondered aloud.

"From condemnation," Genellsteen answered passionately. "As people we are not perfect. We make mistakes; we sin. If we are saved and these sins are forgiven by God, then when we die we will go to paradise, and, on the day of judgment, we will go to Heaven to be with Him."

Avery nodded to let the man know that he understood.

"But if we are not saved, then we will be condemned to the fiery pit of Hell." Mr. Genellsteen flipped rapidly to another passage and read, "Matthew 13:41-42; *The Son of man shall send forth his angels, and they shall gather out of his kingdom all things that offend, and them which do iniquity; And shall cast them into a furnace of fire: there shall be wailing and gnashing of teeth.*"

Avery felt the fog of confusion beginning to clear strangely, but he was still very puzzled. "What do you mean by saved? How could one man save us all?"

Genellsteen thumbed through a few more pages. "Here. Matthew 18:11; *For the Son of man-* meaning Jesus *-is come to save that which was lost.* Jesus came here to rescue we who are lost." Genellsteen saw that Avery was still very befuddled. "Now, let me tell you some of what Jesus did. He cast out demons and evil spirits from people, He healed the sick, made the blind to see, and the deaf to hear; He worked many miracles on this earth." More flipping of pages. "Matthew 17:22-23; *And while they abode in Galilee, Jesus said unto them, The Son of man shall be betrayed into the hands of men: And they shall kill him, and the third day he shall be raised again. And they were exceeding sorry.*"

"But why would anyone want to kill Him if He was doing all these great things?" Avery blurted in his astonishment.

"Because," Genellsteen went on calmly, "they thought Him a liar, a blasphemer. They did not believe that He was the Son of God. They thought all the miracles He worked were from the devil."

"But couldn't He have made them believe?" Avery insisted.

"He knew what had to be," the older man answered simply. He picked up the Bible and began reading again. "Matthew 26:47-49; *And while he yet spake, lo, Judas, one of the twelve, came, and with him a great multitude with swords and staves, from the chief priests and elders of the people. Now he that betrayed him gave them a sign, saying, Whomsoever I shall kiss, that same is he: hold him fast. And forthwith he came to Jesus, and said, Hail, master; and kissed him.* And so, Jesus was betrayed by Judas, one of His disciples, for just thirty pieces of silver." Mr. Genellsteen paused to let Avery ponder this before going on. "Matthew 27:15-26; *Now at that feast the governor was wont to release unto the people a prisoner, whom they would. And they had then a notable prisoner, called Barabbas. Therefore when they were gathered together, Pilate said unto them, Whom will ye that I release unto you? Barabbas, or Jesus which is called Christ? For he knew that for envy they had delivered him. When he was set down on the judgment seat, his wife sent unto him, saying, Have thou nothing to do with that just man: for I have suffered many things this day in a dream because of him. But the chief priests and elders persuaded the multitude that they should ask*

Barabbas, and destroy Jesus. The governor answered and said unto them, Whether of the twain will ye that I release unto you? They said, Barabbas. Pilate saith unto them, What shall I do then with Jesus which is called Christ? They all say unto him, Let him be crucified. And the governor said, Why, what evil hath he done? But they cried out the more, saying, Let him be crucified. When Pilate saw that he could prevail nothing, but that rather a tumult was made, he took water, and washed his hands before the multitude, saying, I am innocent of the blood of this just person: see ye to it. Then answered all the people, and said, His blood be on us, and on our children. Then released he Barabbas unto them: and when he had scourged Jesus, he delivered him to be crucified."

"What does it mean," he asked when Genellsteen had finished, "to be crucified?"

"In those times," Genellsteen explained patiently, "it was a common form of punishment for murderers, liars, thieves…" Genellsteen let the word hang in the air for a moment. "To crucify someone means to nail them by their hands and feet to a wooden cross and stand it upright for all to see until they die of exposure."

Avery flinched and became very interested in the wood grain of the table.

"They beat and mocked and spat on Jesus Christ, the Son of God, then they crucified Him all because they did not believe. Because He brought to the world a new testimony of God's will."

Avery looked at Genellsteen. "But couldn't He have stopped them?"

The aged man nodded, "He could have."

"Then why didn't He?" Avery suddenly fumed, although he was not sure if he was angry with Jesus or himself. "You said yourself that all people sin; people murder, commit adultery, lie," Avery stopped and added quietly, "steal..." He rested his elbows on the table and put his head in his hands. "Why should He have had to die for our wrong doing?"

Mr. Genellsteen laid a hand gently on Avery's back. "That is the measure of God's love for us. He gave His only Son that we might be saved."

Avery looked up with dampened eyes and cheeks.

"Dry your eyes, Avery," Mr. Genellsteen said and handed him a handkerchief. "I have more to tell you. After Jesus died, His body was given to Joseph of Arimathea and he placed it in a tomb. The scribes and Pharisees sealed the tomb up because Jesus had prophesied and said, *After three days I will rise again.* when He still lived. Now," he took up the Bible once more, "listen to this. Matthew 28:1-7; *In the end of the sabbath, as it began to dawn toward the first day of the week, came Mary Magdalene and the other Mary to see the sepulcher. And, behold, there was a great earthquake: for the angel of the Lord descended from heaven, and came and rolled back the stone from the door, and sat upon it. His countenance was like lightning, and his raiment white as snow: And for fear of him the keepers did shake, and became as dead men. And the angel answered and said unto the women, Fear not ye: for I know that ye seek Jesus, which was crucified. He is not here: for he is risen, as he said. Come, see the place where the Lord lay. And go quickly, and tell his disciples that he is risen from the dead; and, behold, he goeth before you into Galilee; there shall ye see him: lo, I have told you."*

Avery seemed pleased with this and he sat for a while trying to fathom a love that strong. Finally he said, "How do I do it?"

"Hm?"

"How do I become saved? Is there something I must do, or does it just happen?"

"In Mark 16:16 Jesus said, *He that believeth and is baptized shall be saved; but he that believeth not shall be damned.*"

"Believe what?"

"That Jesus Christ is the Son of God and that he died for you." Genellsteen still spoke calmly, but Avery's mind was beginning to race.

Avery nodded seriously. "And what is 'baptized'?"

"It means that the person is submerged in water for the remission of sins."

Avery raised an eyebrow in doubt. "You want me to take a bath?"

Genellsteen chuckled, "Mercy, no. It's not a bath." He thumbed through some pages and read, "1 Peter 3:21; *The like figure whereunto even baptism doth also now save us (not the putting away of the filth of the flesh, but the answer of a good conscience toward God,) by the resurrection of Jesus Christ:.*"

Avery sat quietly for a time before stating his conclusion. "So when we are baptized all our sins are forgiven; like beginning again?"

Genellsteen nodded with a soft look of pleasure. "It is being reborn spiritually."

Avery gazed at the Bible. He had a sudden need to learn all that he could from it. He understood that he was a sinner destined for an eternity of torment. But there was still hope. "What else do I need to know?" he asked without lifting his sight from the Book.

Mr. Genellsteen held it out to him. "The teachings in this Book, the Word of God."

Crickets chirped and the wind whispered through the night as Avery sat by the window pouring over the Bible in his lap. Mr. Genellsteen sat snoring in his chair by the fire. Avery's mind was far from asleep as he drank in page after page. He had not stopped since the moment he had accepted the book from Mr. Genellsteen's grasp. Now he understood what Tom and Gilly had been trying to tell him; now he understood why Mia had refused him; now he understood what he must do.

Avery closed the Bible and set it aside. He reached over and shook Mr. Genellsteen lightly. "Hm?" the man grunted before he came fully awake. He sat up straight at the sight of Avery's earnest look.

"Sir," Avery began quietly, "will you baptize me?"

Avery shivered involuntarily as he knelt in the rushing stream water. Mr. Genellsteen stood over him and Todd sat on the bank smiling happily at the proceeding. Gray tendrils of haze surrounded them and the breeze whispered of the coming dawn.

Mr. Genellsteen placed a hand on Avery's shoulder and young Smith gazed up at the starry sky. "Do you believe that Jesus is the Son of God?"

"I do," Avery whispered in a voice tight with emotion.

The grip of the hand on his shoulder tightened. "I baptize you in the name of the Father, the Son, and the Holy Spirit."

Avery felt Mr. Genellsteen clamp a handkerchief over his nose and mouth. And then he was falling back with a cascade of water flowing over his entire body. It seemed as though the world had stopped spinning as he lay there. Eyes wide open, he stared up through the clear water at the clouds above. The sky was filled with swirling storm clouds for a moment. Lightning lept from cloud to cloud. Then they parted and disappeared. In the midst of a brilliantly blue sky, he saw a single, sparkling star.

In a rush of water and chilling wind, Avery felt himself lifting up out of the water. He was shivering in his damp shirt and trousers, but he could not stop himself from smiling. Avery felt like a young child again, seeing everything for the first time. Then he was enveloped by Mr. Genellsteen's strong arms. As he looked over the man's broad shoulder, he watched as the sun began peaking over the horizon in rays of dazzling light.

At a distance he could hear Todd's soft young voice ringing out through the mist.

"Amazing grace, how sweet the sound, that saved a wretch like me..."

For the first time in a long time, Avery felt completely at peace.

"I'm going to Lancashire tomorrow," Avery declared over dinner later that day.

"Oh?" Mr. Genellsteen said with a raised eyebrow.

It was the first time Avery had stopped smiling since dawn. "There's something about my past that I must remedy."

"You're going to turn yourself in?" Todd piped up.

Avery looked up in surprise. Todd blushed and looked down at his plate.

"They came looking for you after you left," Mr. Genellsteen explained. "They showed us a drawing of you."

Avery sighed, "I'm sorry I didn't tell you before. And yes, I am going to turn myself in."

"But why!?" Todd blurted.

"Because I don't want to spend the rest of my life running from someone I used to be." Avery flipped open the Bible to a page he had marked. "Proverbs 6:30-31; *Men do not despise a thief, if he steal to satisfy his soul when he is hungry; But if he be found, he shall restore sevenfold; he shall give all the substance of his house.*"

Mr. Genellsteen nodded solemnly.

That night, Avery sat in the chair by the fire and prayed for the first time in his life. *Lord, grant me the strength to accept and do Your will. I thank You for helping me to find the truth.* Avery went on praying until he drifted asleep. He had no dreams that night, but slept soundly and awoke refreshed.

Todd packed Avery's sack with provisions while he saddled Pinpoint. Father and son stood in the yard with Avery as the sun came fully over the horizon. "Good luck to you, Avery Smith."

Avery nodded and shook Genellsteen's thick hand. Then he turned to the anxious-looking boy.

"But sir," Todd insisted, "what if they should hang you?"

Avery smiled and ruffled the boy's hair fondly. *"He shall cover thee with his feathers, and under his wings shalt thou trust: his truth shall be thy shield and buckler.* I believe it was in Psalms."

Avery swung into the saddle and waved one last time to the Genellsteens. The two smiled and waved back. *Perhaps I shall bring Mia to meet them some day,* he thought oddly. This brought another thought to his mind. "Mr. Genellsteen, may I ask another favor?"

"Of course."

"Will you write to Amelia Bairns in Echo Falls, Ireland and tell her that I was saved?"

Mr. Genellsteen nodded solemnly and raised his hand toward him. Avery turned Pinpoint around and galloped away with a light heart.

Chapter 9
The Gallows

Avery pulled back on the reins and Pinpoint halted with a grateful snort. Letting his cloak hood slide back onto his shoulders, he gazed at the woods on either side of the dusty road. This was the place where he was captured and taken to jail. This was the spot where his life had changed forever. Avery closed his eyes and murmured a silent prayer for strength.

He leapt to the ground and tugged at Pinpoint's reins. "Come on." He trudged along in heavy silence as he watched Lancashire draw closer.

The creaking of wheels and the clop of numerous hooves warned him of an approaching carriage. Avery stepped aside as the carriage, led by a team of high-stepping grays, passed by. Then, unexpectedly, the coach stopped a few feet up the road and the door swung open. An older, stubby man stuck his head out.

"You look like you could use some help, young fellow," he called to Avery.

"Thank you, but no," Avery replied and took a few steps closer. "I'm just on my way to the Lancashire jail."

"Oh?" The man looked down his nose at Avery curiously. "Why's that?"

"I'm turning myself in," Avery answered bluntly. After all, he had no reason, nor was he willing to lie any more.

The man was clearly taken aback. "Well," he stammered, "good luck." He started to shut the door, but stopped when Avery called out to him.

"Wait!" Smith held out his hand. "Sir, would you take me horse? I doubt that I shall need him in...in prison." The man stared blankly at him. Avery led Pinpoint forward so he could look the horse over. "He's a very obedient animal," Avery insisted. "His name is Pinpoint." He took a long breath to try and loosen his constricting throat.

The man raised an eyebrow. "How much?"

"I'm giving him to you," Avery choked out pleadingly. He was suddenly anxious for the man to be gone.

He nodded solemnly. "Tie him to the back."

Avery turned to do the old man's bidding. He retrieved the bag from the saddle horn and stroked Pinpoint's smooth muzzle. He let his fingers linger on the white spot between the animal's curious eyes. "Good bye old friend." He closed his eyes tightly and leaned his forehead against Pinpoint's cheek. The carriage door slammed and the driver cracked his whip. Avery stepped back and watched his beloved Pinpoint trot away.

Avery slung the sack over his shoulder and forced himself forward. He shook his head lightly, trying to focus his thoughts on his destination. He came to the edge of the city and the dirt road turned to cobblestones. He maneuvered through alleys and back roads, unaware of the bustling people around him. He was so sure of what he was about to do, and yet terribly frightened by it. Some faded memory of himself as a child pushed its way into Avery's thoughts. He saw himself wandering through the streets being jostled by strangers. He remembered stealing apples as a boy, then picking pockets as a young man. And then he thought of his mother when she was young and beautiful. That was before they had become destitute. Avery had a single memory of the grand home he had once lived in. He remembered lying on a red rug in the library where he read for hours at a time.

Before he could blink—and much sooner then he liked—Avery stood in front of the heavy jail door. All memories flew away as swiftly as they had come and he crashed back to the present. "Your will be done, Lord," he whispered and gripped the latch. With great effort, he pushed the door inward and stepped over the threshold.

There were no windows, so the small room was lit by two torches. This added darkness did not help Avery's depressed mood. A man, devoid of hair on his crown, sat behind a wide desk directly in front of Avery. "'ere for a visit?" he sneered without looking up from some parchments he was studying.

"Not exactly." Avery swallowed and walked to the edge of the desk. "I'm…that is…I wish to turn myself in."

The man now peered up at him suspiciously. "Who are yew?"

A warm peace swept through Avery and he knew he was certainly doing the right thing. "Avery Smith...the Rapscallion."

The man gave him a strange look. "Think you're being funny, do you?" he said sarcastically and bent back over his work.

Another guard walked in from a side door. "What's this then?"

The balding man pointed at Avery. "He's trying to turn 'imself in as the Rapscallion."

The guard cackled. "Can't be. That boy died months ago. Slain by an arrow from one of our men." He studied Avery in an amused sort of way. "Though you do look a bit like him, he was much older."

Avery felt his cheeks burn. "But he wasn't killed."

"Oh, aye?" the guard demanded. "If one of our soldiers said he killed 'im then he's dead, an' that's an end of it."

"Where's the body?" Avery half laughed.

"Oh the body was washed away in the river where 'e was slain."

"Aye, but I reckon the soul wishes it were in a cooler climate, eh mate?" the man at the desk jeered.

"Judge not lest ye be judged." Avery's words stunned them to silence for a moment.

"What's your name?" the guard scowled irritably.

Avery gave his head a little shake. "Smith, Avery Smith." He almost laughed with relief. If they thought the Rapscallion was dead, then he was free; he had no record under his real name.

Thief of the Gallows

"Sounds familiar."

The man behind the desk shrugged. They both gave Avery searching looks. The guard leaned down and whispered something in the other man's ear. The balding man's head snapped around and he began whispering fervently to his comrade. After some debating from both men, the one behind the desk recovered his uncaring, superior composure.

"Oh yeah," the guard suddenly exclaimed. "Wasn't he the chap with the debts?"

Avery's joy melted away as the man behind the desk produced a wrinkled bit of parchment. "Smith here owes 3,000 pounds to the Lancashire tax collector."

"I *what!?*" Avery exploded.

"You can either pay up," the man explained dryly, "or hang in the square tomorrow."

"*Tomorrow!?*" Avery's body went rigid and his mind went numb.

"Yeah. We got the gallows all set for a murderer, so unless you can pay, you're going after him."

"No, wait," Avery tried to explain as the guard grabbed his arm. "There's been a mistake!"

"Come on," the guard said calmly. "You turned yourself in, you knew what was goin' to happen."

Avery was too stunned to struggle as he was led to a cell. Unlike the last time, they did not shackle him to the wall. He was shoved in and the door slammed shut behind him. He sat in a heap on the floor and gripped at the bits of straw strewn all around him. The two men must have planned their little charade during their whispered conference. Avery had not been allowed to see the document they had held up before them, so it was most likely fake. It might even have been blank.

Avery looked around the cell with a vague feeling of deja-vu. It was not until he turned to the wall at his right that he realized why. He stood up and made his way toward it. On the wall, where once upon a time there had been a window, there was a concrete block wedged in place between the stones. The block was too short for the opening and Avery could easily slip his long fingers through on either side of it. He let his hands drop to his sides heavily. Avery's forlorn face manipulated into a ludicrous smile and he laughed aloud at the irony of it all until tears spilled from his eyes.

"Lord," he prayed aloud, "what manner of cruelty is this?"

Why are ye fearful, O ye of little faith?

The laughter died on Avery's lips as the words echoed in his heart. He prayed until sleep descended upon him, knowing that he could trust in God to save his soul.

Avery stood in a rickety cart beside the murderer. With their hands tied behind their backs, they said not a word as the cart was pulled through the street. Hordes of people, the citizens of Lancashire, crowded around the street shouting insults at the doomed men. Some even threw rotten vegetation at them. Avery stood in his rags ashen faced through the whole ordeal, as if he could not see or hear the people around him. His mind was completely blank and he had himself half convinced that it was all some bizarre dream. It was not until they reached the square that he came out of his trance. Avery saw the crude gallows that had been erected in the middle of the square. The morning sun shone upon the wooden structure. The hangman's noose swayed in the breeze.

The cart creaked to a halt and the two men looked at one another for the first time. Several pairs of hands roughly jerked the murderer down and led him up the few steps to where the noose awaited him.

Avery heard the cheers of the crowd and the beating of the soldiers' drums vividly now. A thin man in a green velvet suit unrolled a sheet of parchment and stood on the platform before the crowd. "Morgan Benter, you are charged with and found guilty of the murders of-" Here there followed a short list of names which Avery had no interest in hearing. "-and have therefore been sentenced to be, on this day, hung by the neck until dead." The man rolled up the parchment and stepped aside. A masked man, which Avery recognized clearly as the hangman, came forward. He slipped a black hood over Morgan Benter's head. He cinched the rope tight around the murderer's throat. Avery turned away, determined that he would not die with the image of a man dangling from a rope in his mind.

There was a loud clatter and the crowd jeered and pointed. After what seemed like an eternity, the guards removed the noose from Benter's neck and dropped his corpse into the cart beside Avery. He stared wide-eyed at the hooded carcass with a sharp pang of fear.

As the men grabbed him and pulled him onto the platform, he tried to calm himself with one thought. *It will all be over soon.*

The man in green stood beside him and unrolled another sheet of parchment. "Avery Smith, you have failed to pay your debts of three-"

"*Stop!*"

Avery looked out at the hushed crowd frantically in an attempt to find the source of the shout while the man in green read on.

"-pounds to Alfred Larc, tax collector of-"

"*You've got the wrong man!*"

"-Lancashire and have been sentenced to be, on this day, hung by the neck until dead."

The beat of the drums quickened. A hood was thrown over Avery's head and he held his breath. *It will all be over soon.* He felt the noose tighten around his throat.

"He can pay his debt! You must listen!" The shouts were closer this time and there were loud footsteps on the stairs of the gallows.

But it was too late. The trapdoor beneath him crashed open and Avery plunged downward.

Chapter 10
Avery Smith Sr.

Avery sat straight up in the bed. His face was drenched in sweat and his breathing came in heavy gasps. He stared around the room, his mouth gaping open in shock.

He was sitting on a four poster bed covered by an intricately patterned quilt. The walls were a pale shade of yellow and the two windows had white lace curtains. On one wall was a painting in a gold frame. In one corner was a mahogany writing desk and in the opposite corner a matching dresser. Avery saw that his sack was sitting on the polished wood. Hanging over the dresser was a mirror. Smith stared at his reflection dumbly. His ragged clothes looked completely out of place in the elegant bedroom. But the part of his reflection that held his attention fast was the ugly, purple bruise on his neck. The puffy abrasion encircled his strong neck. Avery ran his right index finger along it and the fact that he was still alive began to seep into his mind.

"Thank you, merciful God," he breathed joyfully.

Knock, knock, knock!

The short raps on the bedroom door made Avery jump. The door creaked open and an old man walked in. Avery gasped; it was the man he had met on the road into Lancashire.

"Well, I see you're awake, Mr. Smith," he greeted rather sheepishly. He wore an array of finery and a powdered wig. His fancy tailcoat and breeches were a watery shade of blue. Avery stared and after a moment the man laughed nervously. "Come now, surely you remember me?"

"Yes. I gave you my horse," Avery answered simply.

The man shook his head. "I am more than that, lad." He gave Avery an expectant look, but when he said nothing the man shrugged. "You don't recognize me, of course. It has been nine years after all."

Avery blinked and felt his head begin to spin. "U-uncle?"

"That's right," he grinned. "Marcus Lowell."

Avery was not sure how he felt about his uncle at the moment; however, he was more interested in something else. "How did I get here?"

"The guard cut the rope just after the trap door fell. I paid your debt."

"Wait a minute, that wasn't my debt!" Avery insisted hastily.

"Calm down lad." Marcus reached out as if to place a hand on Avery's shoulder but seemed to think better of it. He let his hand drop to his side. "I know that. They mistook you for someone else."

"Who?" Avery was beginning to get a headache as well as a sore throat. "Who could they possibly mistake me for?"

"Your father." Marcus moved to the painting in the gold frame. "This was your father."

The man had been around the age of twenty-two when the portrait had been made. Avery studied the man and realized that he had inherited his father's raven hair. They even looked a little alike in the face, with the exception that Avery's father had a long scar running down one cheek. The man had a look of severity about him, as though he were angry at everyone. Then Avery noticed the woman sitting on a velvet stool beside his father.

"And this, of course," Marcus gestured to the lady, "is-"

"My mother." Avery stood shakily and moved toward the painting. Lorain Smith looked about twenty, her brown tresses resting on her shoulder in a mass of curls. Her gray eyes seemed to dance. Her full lips were painted in a lovely smile, unlike her husband, who's mouth remained straight. Avery reached up to touch her hands that were folded in her lap.

"Father?" someone called from the hall. Avery and Marcus both looked to the door. "I've just heard-" A man walked in but stopped short. He looked older than Avery with a few locks of gray showing through his blond hair. "You!" he sneered at Avery. "I thought you were dead."

"I know you," Avery said vaguely. "You're the one that had me arrested that day."

The man turned to Marcus. "You should have let him hang, Father. He's a liar and a thief!" He pointed an accusing finger at Avery, who flinched in spite of himself.

"He is not a thief, Erin," Marcus fumed suddenly.

"Not any more," Avery corrected.

"He's your cousin." Erin shot Avery a glance filled with loathing. Avery was every bit as surprised as Erin seemed to be. "Now go and tell Mrs. Lela to send up some clean clothes."

Erin turned to leave but Avery called him back. "Erin?" Avery's cousin turned and glared at him. Avery did his best to smile. "Thank you, for having me arrested."

Erin Lowell spun on his heel and stormed away. Marcus turned his attention back to Avery. "Why on earth would you *thank* him for getting you caught and hanged!?"

"Because," he explained simply, "that was the event that changed the course of my life. If I hadn't been thrown in jail, I would not be where I am today."

After a moments awkward pause, Avery raised an eyebrow. "I never knew you had a son."

Marcus shrugged in defeat. "I kept the two of you from meeting on purpose."

Now Avery shrugged. "He's probably just irritated at discovering that he's related to a poor man." He turned back to the painting.

"Lorain was a wonderful person," Marcus breathed. "She deserved more than she got."

"Aye." Avery kept his face turned to the portrait. "So I am named after my father?"

"I thought you knew," Marcus mumbled.

Avery shook his head. "So it was *his* debt that they were going to hang me for."

Marcus sat down on the edge of the bed. "Lorain was promised to Smith from the time she was eighteen. After our mother died, Father really took no interest in her. He didn't know how to raise a girl." Lowell stopped when Avery turned to him with a grave face.

"So he gave her to the first suitor that came calling?"

"The first *rich* suitor. Your father was very fond of gambling. He squandered away his fortune and then-" Avery's uncle paused, unsure whether or not he should be telling him all of this. "Smith died of the plague one winter in France. I believe you were-"

"Nine." Avery sat on the bed beside his uncle. He knew this half of the story. "I never saw more than a glimpse of my father. He was always away in London or France or somewhere. One day he left and never came back. I remember I was three." He was suddenly lost in the vague reverie. "I remember I was in the study—where I wasn't supposed to be—and I heard my mother. She was crying. I went to the door to see what was happening, curious child as I was. I saw the two of them standing in the front doorway. My mother fainted because she was upset that he was leaving, I thought. He caught her as she slumped against him. I remember I had to bite my lip to keep from laughing when he kissed her forehead; I don't know why I found it so hilarious. And he lifted her up and laid her on the chaise lounge in the hall. Then he just stood there, looking at her for the longest time. Suddenly he turned to me and smiled. The man smiled. And then he walked out the door, out of our lives. Forever." Avery grinned weakly. "Mother told me he died in a duel."

"She wanted you to have someone to look up to." Marcus shook his head. "Lorain deserved so much more."

"Aye. But why," Avery asked incredulously, "why didn't she ever come back to her family for help when she...*we*... lost everything?"

"Would you come back to a father who had married you off to the first wealthy scoundrel he met at a dinner party?"

"And you?"

Marcus rubbed at his eyes. "When Father died, he left everything to Lorain. I guess it was his way of apologizing for what he had forced her to do. I blamed her for that because I thought that I should have gotten it all. But she never claimed her inheritance. Then one night, she arrived with you on my doorstep. I had my personal physician tend her. He diagnosed the tuberculosis. Two days later..." Marcus did not finish; he did not need to. Avery sniffed and looked down at his hands. Some part of him had always known that his father was not the man his mother made him out to be. Hearing the notion spoken as fact came as no surprise. "All this is yours now," Marcus said suddenly.

"What?"

"The money, the estate," he faced his nephew. "It would have been yours long ago, but you ran away before I could bring myself to give it to you."

Avery's mouth dropped open once again. "I-I can't accept all this!"

At that moment, a maid walked in bearing a stack of clean clothes in her arms. She placed them on the dresser, curtsied, and walked away.

"Well," Marcus clapped his hands briskly. "I'll leave you to freshen up. Dinner is at six, but Cook will fix you something if you get hungry before then." He stood up and made his way to the door.

"Uncle Marcus?" Avery called and Lowell turned. "My horse, Pinpoint?"

Marcus grinned. "He's in the stables out back." Marcus shut the door and Avery fell back onto the bed, completely overwhelmed.

"Well, what have you been doing all day?" Marcus asked as Avery entered the room. Erin was sitting across from him peering over the edge of his newspaper irritably.

"Sleeping," Avery answered simply.

His uncle gestured to an armchair beside him. With a great rustling of his paper, Erin stood and walked quickly from the room.

Avery watched him go and felt a wrenching in his heart. "I can't stay here," he breathed.

Marcus chortled, "Why ever not, Avery? This is your home; you're a rich man now. Don't let Erin get you feeling that way."

"It's not Erin." Avery looked at Marcus sadly and tried to explain. "My house may be in England, but my life is in Ireland."

Marcus nodded in silent understanding.

"Maybe I'll start a farm of my own." Smith mused. With his elbows on his knees, he rested his chin in his hands.

"What will you do with…" Marcus began quietly.

"I am giving you the estate that you've had all these years." He looked at his uncle happily. "I never wanted it. I'll just take enough with me to get settled in Ireland." He was talking to himself more than Marcus now. But then a strange thought occurred to him. "Uncle?"

"Yes?"

"May I ask you something rather...sensitive?" Marcus simply regarded his nephew curiously. Avery licked his lips. "The day before I left, I heard you in your office. I believe I heard you say, *Send him to an orphanage. He's only a gutter whelp like his mother.*"

Marcus fiddled with the fringe on the arm of his chair. "Had you listened a bit longer, you would have heard me say *right?* with not a little sarcasm."

Avery's eyes watched him searchingly, curiously.

"I never intended to send you away," his Uncle shrugged sadly. "That was what my lawyer—the man you heard me speaking to—would have had me do. I was going to tell you the next morning about the inheritance, but alas, you had vanished."

Avery nodded. Of course. They sat in silence for a time after that, each enveloped in his own thoughts.

"I'll leave for Ireland as soon as I get the chance," Smith finally said.

"Do what you must, Avery."

"No," Avery sighed. "I've done what I must all my life in order to survive. Now I will try my best to do things according to God's will and not my own. I will no longer serve myself, but God." Avery smiled at his uncle fondly. "And I do it gladly."

Avery shut the door of the carriage and went to check that the horses were hooked up properly. Pinpoint nudged at his shoulder fondly and Avery slipped him a sugar cube. The white horse beside Pinpoint neighed softly.

"All right Carmel, all right." Avery gave the large mare her share of the sugar as well.

Carmel had been a gift from Marcus along with the carriage. Avery had used a small portion of his inheritance to buy himself a new wardrobe, which was packed in a trunk in the back of the coach. Buried beneath the clothes was a substantial amount of gold. Ms. Manny's Bible rested on the top.

Avery turned to Marcus and the disgruntled Erin. "I guess that's everything."

Marcus held out his hand. "Your mother loved you very much, Avery."

Young Smith shook his uncle's hand heartily. "Thank you for everything. I owe you my life." Marcus chuckled merrily at the remark. Avery turned to Erin and held out his hand. "Good bye, cousin." Erin's expression remained stern, but he gripped Avery's hand. Avery even thought he saw a smile flicker over the man's features.

Avery climbed into the driver's seat of the carriage and flicked the reins. "Take me home."

Chapter 11
The Echo of the Falls

The gleaming carriage pulled right up to the Haddley's front porch. Tom and Gilly emerged, one looking curious and the other very suspicious. It was not until they saw Avery leap down from his seat that Tom's face broke into his familiar smile.

"Avery!" He called as he hurried down the steps. "Where've ye been now?"

"I did it, Tom!" Avery gripped Tom's shoulders joyfully. "I'm saved!" He immediately began babbling about his stay with the Genellsteens.

"Avery," Gilly said slowly, "Mr. Genellsteen wrote to Mia. He said ye were hung." Avery's happiness dimmed for an instant at the memory. "We thought ye were dead."

"No more than you are now." Avery grasped Gilly's hand with a hearty laugh.

"Come inside," Tom insisted, "have dinner wit' us."

"I can't," Avery answered, the smile never leaving his face. "I have to find Mia." He began unhooking Pinpoint from the coach. "I just had to tell you the good news first. Will you look after Carmel while I'm gone?"

"Of course," Tom nodded and stroked the mare's mane.

Avery retrieved his saddle from the back of the coach and in minutes he was ready to head to town.

"Avery!" Tom hollered with a characteristic grin, "ye're goin' to need thes." Tom held up Avery's diamond ring.

Avery clapped a hand on Tom's shoulder gratefully and accepted the ring. He turned and leapt into the saddle. Taking a deep breath, he went to find his beloved.

Knock, knock!

Avery waited with baited breath but was only slightly disappointed when Ian Bairns answered his raps. "Good afternoon, Mr. Bairns."

Ian's eyes twinkled in mild surprise. "Good day, Mr. Smith."

"Sir," Avery began quietly, "I have come to tell you all that I have found Jesus. I have been saved and devised a means of income for myself; also, I-" he swallowed, "I would like to ask your permission to request Ms. Amelia's hand in marriage."

"Ye mean like ye should have done the first time?" Ian remarked rather harshly.

Avery lowered his eyes to study his hands ashamedly. "Yes, sir."

"Sit down, Mr. Smith." He motioned to two chairs on the porch. "A will admit," he continued as Avery sat down anxiously beside him, "that after speaking with you twice,

A did not like the sound of ye. It will take some convincing for me to give ye the answer ye want to hear." Avery nodded stiffly, inwardly praying for wisdom. Ian rubbed at his chin, "Now, explain to me everything that has happened since ye left."

Avery talked with Ian Bairns for an hour. When the talking was finished, they stood and shook hands. Avery pulled himself slowly onto Pinpoint's back and rode into the forest behind the Bairns household. The weight of Ms. Manny's Bible was light in his pocket.

Mia sat on a boulder, the same boulder where she had once heard a proposal, with her two young cousins. Benny was six and Ann was seven and Mia loved them like brother and sister. Ann sat beside Mia while Benny stood casting stones into the stream. The water of the falls fell in torrents, muffling all sounds of the forest except Mia's voice as she read.

"Blessed are the poor in spirit: for theirs is the kingdom of heaven. Blessed are they that mourn: for they shall be comforted. Blessed are the meek: for they shall inherit the earth. Blessed are they which do hunger and thirst after righteousness: for they shall be filled. Blessed are the merciful: for they shall obtain mercy. Blessed are the pure in heart: for they shall see God. Bless-"

"Blessed are the peacemakers: for they shall be called the children of God." Avery finished and stepped forward. "Matthew 5:9." Mia turned sharply at the sound of his voice. Their eyes locked and Mia could not bring herself to look away.

"Children," she whispered absently, "there are some peppermint sticks in meh saddlebag. Why don't ye go and get them." The two young ones had been studying Avery curiously, but now they rushed gleefully to Mari. Avery smiled down at them when they passed but when he turned his attention to Mia, the smile melted.

"A-" she stammered with tears glistening in her eyes, "A thought ye were hung."

Avery stepped closer. "I was." To his immense surprise his voice sounded strong and sure in the afternoon sunlight. He pulled down the collar of his blue tunic and showed her the grim bruise. She flinched. "But I was saved by a man I once hated."

"Et sounds as though there's a long story behind that," Mia murmured absently.

Avery sat down on Mia's left side. Mia shifted so that her Bible moved as well and closed itself. Avery pulled his own Bible from his pocket. "I suppose you know that I've been doing some reading," he said simply.

"Mr. Smith, may A see that for a moment?" Mia asked suddenly. Avery handed her the Book and she set her own aside. Avery watched Amelia run her fingers over the name. "Avery," she breathed, "this is my Aunt's Bible. How did ye get it?"

Avery felt the weight of astonishment in his mind. "I was with her when she died. Ms. Manny handed me the Bible and said, 'Fly away, Avery'." Another thought occurred to him and he asked, "Why didn't I meet you at Ms. Manny's house before I went to the market that day?"

"It was my mother and A who had gone to visit her," she sighed wistfully. "Our transport was a day late and we didn't want ta worry Aunt Manny, so we stayed in town to wait for it."

Avery nodded and looked to the falls. "I've been doing some reading," Avery repeated. "Two days after I ran away, I was baptized."

"A know," she mumbled. "A friend of yours, Mr. Genell-Genellsteen? He wrote me. A was so happy, A could scarce believe et. Then A read…" She stopped, unable to finish at first. "We all thought…"

"Yes," he answered gruffly. "Yes, I suppose you did. I thought I would be by the time you received the message."

Amelia looked into his eyes then. "Why did ye come back? After everything that had happened?"

Avery gazed at her as well. "You have placed me on my path, Mia. Were it not for you, I never would have wondered about the scripture; I never would have cared. And I-" Mia let out a small gasp and Avery continued. "I couldn't love you more deeply than I do at this moment."

"A-" Mia murmured. "It's almost too good to believe."

Avery let out a small laugh. "Didn't I tell you I would always love you?" Avery fumbled in his pocket and brought out the ring. "I have spoken with your father and he has consented…" Avery let his voice trail away and gazed at her. "I beg you to say yes." He spoke the words so softly that he was sure she had not heard.

Amelia moved her stare toward the ring in his hand. "A was once afraid A would fall into this." She raised a hand

and moved it toward his. "And now A fly to it." Mia slipped her finger into the ring. Avery gripped her shoulder gently with his strong hand, and for the first time Amelia's lips brushed Avery's in a soft kiss.

"Oooooo!" There was an eruption of giggles from behind them. They turned to see the children watching them with pink-lipped smiles and sticky fingers.

The laughter of four carefree people pealed out through the forest and mingled with the echo of the falls.

Epilogue

Dear Uncle Marcus,

I found my life again. Amelia Bairns and I are to be married in the fall. I bought some land outside of Echo Falls and a small farm is being built there even as I write this. I took Amelia to Dublin to purchase her wedding dress, but she insists on not letting me see it until the wedding.

I invite you and Erin to come. It would be wonderful to see you both again.

I would like to discuss the subject of Christianity with you also, Uncle. I got the impression that either you don't have it, or you keep it at arm's length. If this is indeed the case, I implore you to seek it. The Bible holds all the answers. Salvation awaits you, Uncle.

Until we meet again, God bless you.

Sincerely,
Avery Smith

Printed in the United States
81618LV00001B/289-315